Brumbletide
and the
Rise of the Firebreather

J. Reese Bradley

Illustrations by Brynn Miller

Table of Contents

Magnus
Hildi
Fergus
Teddy
Theory
Zelda
Brynn Miller, age 11

Brynn Miller, age 11

Brynn Miller, age 11

Brynn Miller, age 11

Brynn Miller, age 11

Chapter 1:
Long Live Michelle

A red velvet carpet seems to go on forever but ends at a glorious purple throne on a red dais. I step slowly toward it keeping my head high and eyes fixed ahead. The cheers of my subjects crowded in the Throne Room thrill me, but I dare not show it. Someone holds the train of my robe; maybe the servant who helped bathe me for the event—I don't remember his name or face. The cheers grow louder and more admiring the closer I get to my throne.

"Michelle! Michelle! Long live Michelle!"

But blaring through it all is one unmistakably queer voice in the congregation, louder than all the others and high like a scream. It grows louder and queerer the closer I get to my throne. Does no one hear it?

The hideous shrill sound sends chills through my skin and I grind my teeth. I will not flinch. Keep toward your throne,

Michelle. But the obnoxious ruckus only grows louder and more severe. With no choice, I turn my head...

I cannot open my eyes from the searing agony radiating through my temples. The sheets of my bed are sticky with ooze from the boils that cover me. I want to vomit, but I am too exhausted, so I only lay in unsettled quease. I haven't eaten in days, anyway. Still, I heave, which in turn sends volts of excruciating pain through every nerve still functioning. The Black Death shows no mercy to its captives.

Another heave brings with it the swim of fever delirium beginning again. I recognize it when it comes but the visions appear so real...

Stepping, stepping, stepping to my throne. Keep in time with the music, Michelle. Shoulders back, head high. The throne is much closer now—cheers roar.

"Michelle! Michelle! Long live Michelle!"

The cheers and chants for me are alone music to my ears. There is no need for instruments, but a king must have them to accompany his saunter. My throne, my glorious throne, shines in splendor now. With every step it glows brighter, welcoming its king. Its gold glitters. Its purple velvet like an amethyst sparkling in the sun. The light from the throne fills the room, the cheers roar louder than ever. Giddy—I am simply giddy! My lips part into a grin—I cannot help it. My foot touches the red velvet dais. My throne. My throne. It is mine. It is mine. And these are my subjects. Mine. They will serve me well. I step up. I turn to face my people.

The voice. The queer voice.

The obnoxious, searing scream has returned louder and more obnoxious than before. My subjects—they are all a blur. All I hear is the queer gong of the shrill, antagonizing voice. What is it? Where is it coming from? What does it say?

All is starting to dim. All is going black. Yet the voice carries on. And before everything is no longer, I hear it speak hideously clear.

"It is I, Michelle. I am you."

Chapter 2:
I'll Kill It

So cold. I blink open my eyes.

Something is different. Very different. Warmth melts my icy veins. I sit up. Alas, when was the last time I sat up?

"What happened?" I ask myself.

"Michelle! Michelle, we are healed! The White Stag has healed us!" My sister, Soleil, is ecstatic—*and well.*

The last time I saw her—this morning? I have no idea—she was on death's door. Now look at her. Her face is pink as a peach, and she is up out of bed.

But I see no stag. "What white stag? Where is it?"

Then suddenly, every one of my senses jolts at the sight of a massive tiger in our bedroom! I run— *run! Unimaginable!* —to my wardrobe and remove a spear our father handed down to me from his time in Africa.

"Michelle! No!" yells my foolish sister.

Our servant bursts into the room. "Master! Great Scott!" He hides behind the door at seeing the beast. "Don't worry, Master! I'll kill it!"

"With what, you fool?"

Suddenly, before our very eyes, the tiger transforms into a woman! Could I still be in mania from the plague?

"Sorcerer!" I shout.

"You!" shouts the servant.

"Me," replies the woman. It speaks! "King Pippin has healed your master and mistress of the plague. But now, they must come with me."

My stupid sister cries tears of joy at the beast's words. "Michelle, oh Michelle, we are well! We must go with her."

I stay right where I am behind my wardrobe and look around the bedroom. What nonsense is she speaking? "I saw no stag."

"He was here! You missed him because...well, because..." Soleil hesitates to finish her statement.

"You were dead," the tiger woman says bluntly.

"How ridiculous. Of course, I wasn't dead. I'm standing right here, alive. Dead! Nonsense."

"Come with me," says the woman with complete disregard. She walks toward the door, and Soleil follows! How is this naïve idiot my blood relation?

"Brother, come," Soleil pleads like a whining child.

Going with the tiger woman is undoubtedly a dangerous endeavor, but she certainly has miraculous power that wherever she takes us will surely have loads more. I'll go. But at the first sight of danger, I'll kill it.

"I'll come. But only to watch out for you, Soleil. You do such foolish things."

On my way to join them, I swiftly and stealthily grab my knife from my open wardrobe and slip it into my pocket. The woman melts into the tiger again as she leads us down our stairs.

Several times along the way, I change my mind and almost stab the tiger. The only thing keeping me from doing so is her size. The more I watch her, the more I think I cannot compete if she comes at me.

We have gone along the outskirts of town and arrived by the wood. Startling me, the tiger suddenly stops and turns to us. I grasp the knife in my pocket.

"Things will change now. Ready yourself." It's so strange to see the vicious mouth moving and words coming from it. Astonishing.

Shortly after entering the wood, an owl swoops in front of me and Soleil, almost batting me with its wing! I swat at the pesky thing. "Shoo!"

It doesn't seem to notice me. It only begins flying low ahead of us, and I am suddenly aware I am following it. This is a strange bird, this owl. I cannot bring myself to look away. Its wings—the flapping of its majestic wings is mesmerizing...

The stag.

There it is now before us. How queer are these animals! And where are we now? The wood looks nothing like when we entered! Snow is falling and has now covered the trees and ground. Where is all this snow coming from, and how did it accumulate so fast?

The stag doesn't look like anything much, though his white head would certainly be handsome on my wall.

My sister gasps at it and then fixes her eyes above. "Brother! How wonderful! Look at that magic tree!"

What the bloody hell is she blubbering on about? There's nothing but the stag and the snowy wood.

"It isn't magic, foolish sister."

Soleil falls on her knees before the stag and thanks him for things we've not received.

"It is my gift to you, dear one," he replies to her. "Now, come with me to rule a new land I am preparing."

Rule?

"A new land? We will rule it?" I ask suspiciously.

The stag only turns to leave.

I follow because my interest is now too piqued not to. I'll kill him if things go sour. The stag is not a threat like the tiger.

"Wait!" cries Soleil.

The stag stops and turns to her. "What is it, child?"

"I—I cannot go to this place you have made," she blubbers. "I cannot be a ruler."

Of course, you can't.

"I am not worthy, Your Majesty. I am overcome with the compulsion to tell you I have done horrible things."

What is she speaking of? Soleil is good as gold. Does she have secrets?

"They didn't seem horrible until just this very moment, Your Majesty. But I see now that I am unclean before you. I cannot go," Soleil sobs.

Fine, don't go, you idiot girl. The stag is obviously only bringing you because you are my relation.

Then the stag tells Soleil that he knows of the things she has done! How? Has she met him before?

"Uncover your face. I have taken away your shame," the stag tells Soleil.

She does so and finally follows us.

That is how it all began. I remember it as clear as a bell, and now here I sit, cozy and comfortable in my own tower. A King! King Michelle of Firebreather House. But I sit alone in my tower, king of nothing. I have no house—no subjects—and no assurance that I ever will.

I stroke the sleeping dragon who lies by my chair. I look around at the thousands of glorious shelves circling around me, filled with knowledge to devour. It is all a dream come true.

What could I possibly need after all of this? Dear reader, you may think less of me at my next words: I do need more. I need more, as all the great men throughout time needed more. You see, I was born for greatness. I will change the world, and everyone for all generations will remember King Michelle Everly. I must have my *own* kingdom in order to fulfill my destiny. I cannot share it with anyone, let alone people such as these the stag has preposterously chosen. The harlot of the pub! I couldn't believe my eyes when I saw! The stag obviously has no idea of her former life—her beauty has gotten her to this kingdom. But the ignorance of the stag for all the others! Even if I *wanted* to stay, this kingdom fell before it arose simply because of the fools running it. Pippin has power but no brains. The only one that could even possibly be useful is George.

I touch the tips of my fingers together, contemplating my work over the past few weeks. The harlot's husband, Boris, is a sheep and has given his full trust to the lion. Slowly, he has come to trust my plan and will help me lead a hefty congregation into my kingdom.

The fire crackles. A ruby diadem glimmers on a purple pillow from a table by the fireplace. I admire it and grin. The harlot's crown is now mine—only five more to steal. I plan to get them before the coronation. If only that stag would tell us when it will be! I shall certainly be gone before it. The crowns shall surely add power to my kingdom.

Just as I think to myself to hide the ruby crown away—no one believes in locks on the doors here, or even doors for that matter. I do miss the privacy of my old home. I will soon have privacy again—a foot steps out of the fire. I roll my eyes. See?

"I was able to get away for a minute, sir. Sara Lisa is with the baby, so I can't be too long." Boris glances at the ruby diadem that belonged to his wife, and his brow lifts.

"We'll have them all soon, my friend," I tell him.

Boris seems to experience some inner turmoil. I quickly pull him out of it. "Remember, whatever sacrifices you make, a hundredfold better is waiting. This is the future of your boy we are talking about. What kind of future could he possibly have with *women* ruling the land in which he lives?"

"I know, I know. It's just difficult to separate facts from feelings, I guess."

"Ah, yes, but we must. All great men have."

Boris nods.

Excellent.

Brynn Miller, age 11

Chapter 3:
Imbecile

Here I am in paradise, a king with the promise of a kingdom but no proof. I have escaped the throws of the Black Death only to be placed in a kingdom like none other the world has ever seen by a power the world has never known. I thought it before, but now I am certain nothing that happens to me is by chance. The cosmic powers, whoever or whatever they may be—could they perhaps even be myself?—they have ensured I survived and was brought to this prestigious position all to set me on the right path toward my kingdom, the greatest kingdom the world will ever know. And they have set before me servants ready to be brought to their new place of work. Glorious, glorious! I must only be strong and courageous.

"King Michelle."

My breath catches. It's the stag. He has come into my tower silently. He stands in front of the crackling fireplace, looking at the ruby crown that sits on the carved coffee table like a chandelier on a log. How could I have been so foolish as not to put it away immediately?

"Your Majesty, I can explain—"

"You are missed at High Noon Fair. Please make haste to join us." He mentions not the diadem.

"Yes, Sire, time has gotten away from me. I'll come now."

"Very good." And with that, he vanishes through the fireplace.

He didn't notice the ruby crown? Of course, he didn't. There are a million crowns in this place. In The Resplendent alone are thousands, I'm sure! Of course. It could be any old crown.

Before heading down, I give myself the once over in a looking glass in my office (that everyone has access to. This *will* change.)

My black onyx crown on my white hair is stunning. It commands attention as a king's crown should. I smile at handsome King Michelle before leaving the closet and going through the flames of the fireplace to board the carpet the Snickerlings have brought. We soar up and up as the conical roof of the tower creeks open, revealing the puffy cumulus clouds of the noon sky. The dragon awakes and follows. Why must he go everywhere I do? This will change as well.

In the Throne Room, the other "royals" sit around the magnificent feast, squalling about something.

"You must be careful, Sara Lisa. A queen must have her crown in sight at all times. Do not lose it again."

On the harlot's head, like a bulbous birthday cake, is a sparkling brand-new coronet with a golden oval on top that looks like it could hold a stone.

The harlot rolls her eyes. "How would *you* know, Justice? Last time I checked, you had no royal upbringing, just as I haven't. And from what I've heard of queens and kings, they do more than watch a crown all day. I was in the bath, for heaven's sake!"

"I'm just saying, be more careful," Justice replies, filling his goblet.

"I'll be more careful too, Sara Lisa," says Soleil. "I'm probably the messiest of the bunch," she laughs with Flori.

"Probably, sister? Certainly," I say, taking a seat by the brut, George, who is accosting a turkey leg like a barbarian.

"Michelle, Sara Lisa lost her crown, and Pippin had to make her a new one!"

I feel my face flush, though I do not flinch. That is, until the stag appears at the head of the table. I don't lift my eyes to his but feel them boring into my soul. But after what feels like an eternity and not of my own free will, I do meet his blazing green gaze that drives into my inner being like a flood. This was all a mistake.

"Everything works together for the good in the end," he says, our eyes still locked.

What does that mean? Why does there seem to be an ominousness in his words? But he is letting me off the hook! Or better, he doesn't know. "Indeed, Sire, indeed," I say, now pouring myself a goblet of crimson liquid.

The more I consider the stag's words, the more ridiculous they sound. Pippin is an imbecile. It is now quite apparent that his power is only being used by those in *true* power to take me where I need to go. Keep moving, Michelle. I fill my plate with eggs and fruit.

The others go on with High Noon Fair, chatting, laughing, and enjoying each other's company. The warmouths flit about happily, and the Snickerlings sing above. The others speak to me, offer me food and drink, ask me questions, and I answer, but I do not listen to them or myself. My mind reels on one thing only—how I will get the stag's map and use it to build my kingdom.

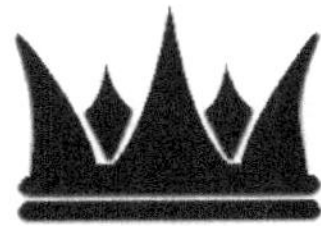

Chapter 4:
Execute

After the feast, Snickerlings fly me to my tower. Sitting amongst the feathery wings, I ponder the stupid playground that is this castle. So much potential wasted on massive teapots, gargantuan gardens, and the strangest of entryways and corridors. Eve seems to notice not that she's gotten nothing in this deal! I hear she has always been out of her mind. Pippin was so foolish to choose *these* to rule with him. The weakest and most despised of the world? What was he thinking?

Two towers from here I shall keep in the plans for my castle: mine and Soleil's. Academics are vital for the proper growth of any given people. Of course, the studies will only be open to a select few.

My tower's conical roof opens, and the Snickerlings and I descend through the shelves and shelves of glorious books. The library will stay the same in my castle. Maybe even a grander library! The ruby diadem is still sitting on the coffee table where I, and surprisingly Pippin, left it. When the Snickerlings are out the roof again, and I hear the thud of its closing, I swiftly pack away the ruby crown in my satchel of things I am taking with me when we go. At High Noon Fair, Pippin informed us that the Coronation would happen soon, so my plans must change. I had hoped to steal the other crowns before leaving, but perhaps I will only have the ruby diadem of the harlot. But all is well. We were told we would receive gifts at the Coronation, so I will attend before making my move. Still, I will certainly be gone before the Inauguration Pippin said would happen shortly after the Coronation. Apparently, this Inauguration ceremony will then leave Brumbletide open to anyone and everyone! Absolutely not. Soon, terribly soon, I and my followers will be gone from Brumbletide forever. I will tell Boris to gather everyone who has listened to our ideas with positive enthusiasm.

There have also been, to my delight, several Snickerlings showing interest as well. I told them to tell their animal counterparts too, since I do not speak the language of the beasts. They say there are a good many willing to come. These are wise creatures; this realm doesn't deserve them.

Pippin requires us to attend at least one of the gorge fests daily, so I will stay in tonight with Boris and inform him of how the plan will be executed after the Coronation.

"Godspeed, Your Majesty," I say to myself. I am proving to be a quite worthy king.

Antlers emerge from the fireplace, and the stag is again in my tower. "King Michelle, may I please have your crown?"

I freeze. He wants the ruby diadem back, after all.

"That one on your head," he says plainly.

"Oh, alright, Your Majesty. For what reason?"

"It's a surprise."

"But will you give it back?"

"I might. I might not."

He can't have it then. But what do I do?

"Just trust me, Michelle," Pippin sounds exasperated. I'm annoying him. It is not wise to be on his bad side before my plan is executed. I'll give it to him. I don't need it anyway. I can make a new one, a better one after my kingdom is built.

I pull the crown off my head and hand it to the stag, who takes it in his teeth. He leaps into the air and bounds up my bookshelves. The conical roof pops open, and the stag leaps out the top of the tower. I stand, mouth agape, in awe of his power.

Chapter 5:
The Coronation

It is the tenth day of the twelfth month. The closer the execution of my plan approaches, the more I hate Brumbletide. Pippin has all but set the crowns of the chosen, mine included, in a chest under the sea so we can't get to them.

In addition, I find that a new area of the castle is gone every time I emerge from my tower. At first, I wondered why the others didn't seem to notice. No one mentioned anything about their tower being gone or different in any way. I became suspicious and eventually asked Soleil if anything was missing, to which she replied that everything was only more real and radiant than when we first arrived. At this point, all that is left is my tower, the Throne Room, and the Remembering Hall.

I am uncertain as to why this phenomenon is happening to me, but it solidifies why I must take this power laid before me and form my kingdom. Another sign from the Powers That Be.

All the Chosen have been called to the Throne Room for what the Snickerlings have said is a special event. As per usual, I am the last one to join the feast. The Throne Room is decorated even more lavishly today. Sparkling garland is strewn from every ledge, banister, and chandelier, and hundreds of candles are lit giving the room a romantic glow. A monstrous fir tree in the middle of the floor reaches to some of the highest balconies. Snickerlings and warmouths lift Boris's brats to decorate the monstrosity with baubles and candies. I have great plans for both the creatures and the children in my kingdom. My lips part into a grin at the thought. Soleil elbows me in the side, her eyes twinkling. "Michelle, I'll be. You're a softy for the lads."

This deserves no response. I spoon pumpkin dumplings into my bowl and grab a bourbon roll. The Snickerlings blow their trumpets, and everyone comes to take a seat at the long table loaded with delicacies. The stag speaks while Snickerlings and warmouths hover around him. I imagine myself in his place.

"Feast! Feast!" Pippin says. "Today is a day of rejoicing. Feast, friends, while the seven Chosen are crowned."

Everyone begins to stuff their bulbous faces. I've always been repulsed watching people eat.

Pippin calls Justice to him. Why would he choose Justice first? I must be going last—the best for last.

From a Snickerling, Justice the Stupid, the town drunk no less, receives his crown that Pippin gave him already. Was something done to them? Another Snickerling places a red stone the color of blood in his crown. He is then given a tiny bird as a helper. What good could the sparrow possibly do him?

The harlot is next. Her new gaudy crown is given one ruby in the golden oval at the top. We are told these stones supposedly give us eternal life. I am relieved that I have stayed for the Coronation. Universe, my thanks! I almost missed another marvelous gift from you to ensure my success—of which now is *eternal* success.

A great beastly cat is given as a helper to the harlot. I recoil as it walks past with its mistress, who joins Boris and their spawn.

My sister and I are called. Nothing has been worse in my life than having to share everything with the twit.

We are both given an onyx stone. Soleil's is white, mine is black. We both receive a dragon helper. Though I only desire the magic from my beast, it is clear that the stag takes me much more seriously as a ruler. Gabriel is strong and fierce, his lungs hot with fire. Soleil's dopey, loping lizard is nothing more than a plaything of sorts with a hanging tongue and wagging tail.

Soleil is given her gifts first and then the best for last—my crown now clings to my head firmly. Something has been done to them, indeed. However, not all is well. The stag blesses Soleil, but he speaks strange words to me—chilling words.

"And you, King Michelle of Firebreather, Son of Destruction, to you is given a crown of black onyx, and your warmouth, Gabriel the purple dragon, will be sacrificed for your deeds."

Startled at his declaration, my brows raise, and I bow, knowing nothing else to do or say. Screams screech from the table as fire is breathed into the room, and my frightful and faithful warmouth joins my side.

I smile at how the Powers of the Universe adorn their future king.

Chapter 6:
Won with Blood

There are more than I thought there would be. Of course, there are. It is easy for anyone to see what is clearly the best path. All except the other "royals" that is. All the spawn: George's son, Justice's daughter, Eve's boy and girl, Boris's students—*all* of the husbands and wives! If there wasn't a sign that I was on the right path before now, here it is.

The only thing I would change is that, along with all his whining pupils, Boris has brought the baby! I thought certainly he would leave it with the harlot. At first, I thought to force him to leave it, but then thought better of it. This baby will be the first to grow up in the new kingdom. *My* people. My *lineage*.

We have all left the Axiom and are now in the Forest Between the Worlds. A storm is brewing, and the sky is deep lavender. A blood moon is shining in the eerie sky at a strange hour. Thunder rolls in the distance.

We have the Digglewip. The shrewd Snickerlings stole it from the stag while he was away. Where he went, none of us know.

He just disappears here and there. How can a king rule his kingdom when he isn't even in it? Surely a reason why the kingdom is falling apart before his very eyes.

I run with the sorcerous map in hand, my subjects behind me, to the edge of the storm. The baby cries. I might do away with it after all.

The waves of the sea crash against the shore, spraying some of us. As soon as we left the Axiom, Brumbletide went dark. We are on our own now, but this is the glorious beginning. When I left, the kingdom was nothing. The Power of the Universe was only using it to further my journey. This is the moment I've waited for my whole life.

Holding the Digglewip with both hands, I shout toward the sea, "We shall call this kingdom Emily, for it will rival all the great kingdoms of the earth!" I hold my breath, waiting for the name to appear on the map just as *Brumbletide* had when Pippin spoke it into existence. Brumbletide is such a ridiculous name.

Nothing happens.

When we left the Axiom, the map, too, went blank just as Brumbletide went dark. This, I saw as a positive—a blank slate to work from. But now I wait for something to happen on the parchment. Nothing.

"What is happening?" I shout in frustration. "Why isn't it working?"

"Perhaps it is because Pippin isn't here?" offers a Snickerling.

"That can't be it! How will we build the kingdom if it won't work without the stag?"

And then, the Universe came to my rescue. They saw my need and swiftly came to my aid.

"We have magic, King Michelle. Maybe we can try," says a small voice.

I stare in awe at the luminescent, white wings all around me. Why has it not occurred to me before that these natural-born servants are also copious sources of power at my disposal? I was too focused on the magic of the stag. I am unable to hold back a smile. "Yes, I would like for you to try, thank you."

But my glee is short lived. It is quickly piqued and then distinguished when even these miraculous creatures cannot summon the necessary magic to create the kingdom. Have I ruined everything? Have I even given up my chance of being a royal at all?

A Snickerlings boy flies to us swiftly from the east.

"Sir, the Chosen of Brumbletide are on their way; armies of Snickerlings and warmouths aligned in battle formation."

Fearing their willingness to fight and knowing their power, I gather the humans to hide behind some brush in the wood with me. We watch.

The remaining Chosen are charging our way with the Horsemen! No one mentioned the Horsemen. What to do? If they defeat the wall of my Snickerlings and warmouths, I will abandon everything and start a new life elsewhere.

The Chosen and Horsemen, along with their Snickerlings, clash with mine, and a great battle ensues. I didn't expect this would happen, but was there ever a great kingdom that wasn't won with blood?

Just as I am pondering these things, my followers—the family of the six others Chosen—get up and go to help them! How easily they are defeated! How easily they betray! Weak-willed fools. The only ones who have stayed with me are Boris's pupils and only to watch his spawn. I should kill them all now. I must do something! It cannot all end now—it hasn't even begun. I hear myself shout to the remaining creatures, "Align, Snickerlings and warmouths of Emily! Attack!"

And to my surprise, they do! My followers, the weak-willed dolts, are a blubbering mess now running around like mice trying without success to stop the battle. Justice's stupid daughter cries, "What have we done? This is all our fault!"

"We have to stop this somehow!" shouts Boris.

Hatred wells up inside of me like rising mercury. "If you aren't for us, you are against us. Snickerlings, ready yourselves to terminate the traitors!"

My followers fall to their weak wills. They run to help their loved ones whom they had settled on abandoning only hours ago. Repulsive. How absolutely disgusting.

As I watch in disgust, I recall a night with two Snickerling boys spent devising this plan and what we might do if it went awry. They told me—I didn't believe them then. It seemed so outlandish.

My rigid nerves go smooth. My shoulders loosen. The Universe has smiled upon me once again. My conversation with the wise Snickerlings weeks ago has come to the forefront of my mind at just the right moment—the conversation we had about what might occur if the worst should arise. I couldn't then imagine it happening on the very *day* of our leaving, but it has.

Calmly, I turn to the Snickerlings I had spoken with. They are by my side, as the Universe has obviously commanded. "What we spoke of, do it now."

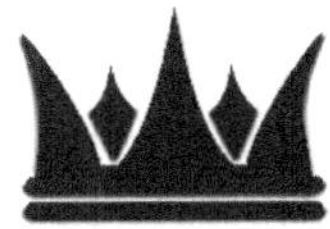

Chapter 7: The Sadness

In silence, I wait and watch. I don't take a breath. A strange sound comes from the Snickerlings—a honking of sorts like a flock of geese. They circle the traitors, and with the peculiar sound pours forth from their small mouths thick, green, twinkling breath. Wonderful—absolutely miraculous! What king has servants like these?

The same edgy sadness wells in my belly. I've felt it many times before. It always comes when I turn over a new leaf—a transition. Or would the word be transformation? Awakening? It came when I killed the family cat. It came the first time I snuck away in the night. It came the first time I gave in to my personal passions (I still can't fully face them.) It came the first time I lied to Father about loving Mother. It came the first time I beat Soleil for her foolish nagging. It came the first time I realized I am not like the other men—that I am meant for greatness and, therefore, must live in solitude even with others.

The feeling is the same every time. The rise of fear, as if there is a choice with life or death at stake, and I must choose at once. And then the beating of the thoughts—beating into submission the gleaming hope of hope. The hope that if I do the fairytale "right thing" all will go well for me. When I fight through this nagging lie and grasp the "other"—the way of greatness—there is always a thrill. I've done it! I've made it to a new height!

But it never fails; the sadness always comes. That pooling of sadness, that heaviness of innocence fading more and more from me. I feel it now. It will pass, but I feel it. Every time, I have the same vision of Mother and Father walking with me in the wood, each holding one of my hands, and I am swinging between them as we walk. Soleil was unwell and back home with the servants, so it was only me with them. But they have been long dead. And that boy swinging between them has died more with each new awakening. These are the sacrifices that must be made for greatness.

The green twinkling breath falls like snow flurries on the traitors who waddle around worriedly, at a loss of how to stop the madness. One by one, each of them stops suddenly as if shocked by lightning. I watch in thrill as their faces go from worry to shock to utter disbelief as they race to save their loved ones, the Chosen, only to strangle and stab and punch and tackle! Their mouths shout "No!" but their bodies disobey and attack.

A laugh escapes me. The Universe has rewarded me again. Look at Boris beating his wife senseless, all the while sobbing like an infant. This only proves that no one is fit to rule this kingdom but me. No one else can keep their emotions controlled.

Snickerlings and warmouths are dropping dead everywhere. But my loyal beast, Gabriel, fights well. Many magical creatures have given their lives for this worthy cause, and I am sure the Universe will somehow reward them.

With the war raging, I am compelled to get back to the sea and try to conjure this kingdom in case all goes south, and I cannot do anything at all. A pack of winged wolves charge the battlefield.

"Friends!" I call.

The wolves stop and look.

"Would you be so kind as to shield a friend?"

The terrifying creatures obey, circling me and tightening in. They extend their magnificent white wings, making a great shield between me and the war.

"To the sea!"

Holding the Digglewip open, I walk the battlefield in the safety of the vicious wolves. Through their legs, I see a slain Snicklering boy—a soldier who died for his master. But as we pass, I notice two things that strike me. The wings of the magical boy illumine brighter than those of the living, and the Digglewip seems to respond. It glows in tandem with the pulsing magic of the dead boy. I grin with glee at this discovery.

"Go to that dead boy," I tell the wolves, and we've enveloped him in no time. The Digglewip shines so brilliantly that I have to squint as I drag the boy with us to the sea.

Suddenly, a screeching like a banshee is behind me, and I am knocked to the ground. My face plants into the dust; I spit mud. What in the name? It's the harlot! She has somehow blasted through the wolves!

"Kill her!" I shout, overcome with annoyance and rage. I am done with the other Chosen. "Kill them all! Do not let the Chosen return!" Immediately, I see this was not a wise demand as now the pack of wolves has dispersed to the Chosen, and only one is against the harlot instead of a horde. Her ruby gleams in her crown—it is giving her a superhuman power. I touch my crown that holds the black onyx. Why is mine not doing the same?

"I'm not dying anytime soon, you repulsive piece of dung!" the harlot shouts. The ruby blasts a beam at me, and I dance out of its way. How is she doing that? Pippin. He must have enchanted their stones after I left.

"Snickerlings!" I shout. "Retrieve each stone from the crowns of the Chosen!"

At once, my army goes after them, and even through the thrilling beams of light that blast from each crown, the Snickerlings overtake them and steal the stones from the stupid sheep. See, this war had to happen. It was all orchestrated by the Universe to ensure I have all I need for my kingdom.

With their stones gone, the Chosen are now fighting in their own power a battle they were losing anyway. Even the Horsemen cannot gain the upper hand. The harlot, who tried to get to me on horseback, is now knocked to the ground by Snickerlings but puts up such a fight that the creatures are unable to retrieve her ruby. Red light blasts randomly here and there, occasionally knocking a Snickerling to the ground. Who knew that of all the Chosen, it would be the harlot who showed the most strength?

As I look on, a mandrill warmouth falls dead at my feet. The mouth hangs open, revealing its massive fangs. I smile; the Universe is always right on time. I seize the mandrill and drag it to the jumble that is the Snickerlings and harlot.

"Stand down!" I command. It brings me great pleasure to aid my servants.

I glare down at the writhing harlot—the sick, silly harlot from the pub. Mandrill in hand, my onyx blazes power through me—I feel it! It's working! There is power to unleash from it, but I do not yet know how to wield it.

The harlot is stunned, unable to get up. It must be my stone doing it. Victory is at hand.

"What is pleasing to the eye can be quite a menace, can it not? Let me make it less of a problem for you." Stepping on her belly, I wrench open wide the mouth of the mandrill and gouge its fang into the harlot's eye. Screaming in agony, she doesn't even seem to realize when the Snickerlings take her stone.

Victory. Sweet victory. But as the sky darkens to black and thunder rolls like an avalanche, I see I will have one more unescapable obstacle before I reach the sea.

Chapter 8:
So Much Blood

The stag. He comes. All is lost. Yet, I will die for my cause.

In the bloody battle, cheers rise from the Chosen, creatures, and Horsemen.

With a voice that almost blows me down, the stag speaks. "Stop killing what is mine."

I choke out my response from a parched throat. "I'm sorry, but the ones who chose to follow me now have no choice but to kill them. It won't be long now."

George's daughter screams while stabbing at her father with a dagger. His wife is choking him. Both women sob apologies the whole time. This sorcery is incredible. Even with the stag here, I am thrilled.

"I don't know how to stop it," I tell the stag. I do not tell him I do not want to stop it.

The stag turns his head toward the sorcery. He seems to ponder the situation. Have I thrown him? Has he no idea what to do? I've ruined his plans. It must feel ridiculous to realize how foolish you are—how loose your plans were! To have them all undone in a matter of hours by one of your own.

"I'll give you the magic you need to do it." The stag looks me in the eyes. For the moment, I am taken aback. The sureness in his gaze makes me uneasy. Leery.

"No!" shouts the drunk. "No, Your Majesty!"

"What would that help?" shouts Eve, running from her children.

I raise my brows. What is the stag thinking? Does he have a plan? One far superior to the foolish one? But looking past him at the war still raging, it is clear there is no plan. All of his plans have failed. Universe, is the stag surrendering to me? I am filled with pride—a magic in my lungs of sheer victory.

"Yes, show me how to stop it."

Pippin trots toward me, and at once, at the prompting of the Universe, the dagger in my cloak comes to the forefront of my mind. I am eye to eye with the beast. I gasp. His eyes, his blazing green eyes, have a sorcery all their own. That edginess, that pit that wells within me every time I step into a new awakening, is heavier than ever. I want to vomit. I close my lips and breathe through my nostrils, composing myself. I want to look away.

"Do quickly what you will," he whispers.

Without hesitation, as if this was my duty from the beginning, my hand shifts to my pocket and finds the dagger I took to kill the tiger. Easily—so easily, I drive it into the stag's heart. Screams. I drive it into him four more times.

He falls, blood pooling around him. It is done.

Panting, I stare at the dead stag. I am overcome with rage for a reason I do not know. I kick the carcass, then grab the great antlers, waiting for the magic to release.

But no glowing comes. Only blood. So much blood. I watch in horror as more blood than one body could ever hold pours from the stag's heart. It floods the battlefield, and not only that, when it touches the feet of the traitors, the Snickerling's enchantment is gone. They stop fighting their loved ones.

"Seize the slaves!" I yell in disbelief. Immediately, my Snickerlings hoist the traitors in the air and race with me to the sea. We hide until the creatures of Brumbletide have gone.

Shaken, I have to work to compose myself. I cannot rid the feeling that there was more to the great wash of Pippin's blood than I realize. It is too peculiar an incident, even in this land where peculiar things are sure to occur. I am uneasy leaving the blood-soaked site.

Still, the Universe has gotten me through it all.

It is time to build my kingdom.

Chapter 9:
Damn it All

With the Digglewip tucked under my arm, I drag the magic boy who had fallen in battle to the sea's edge. Brumbletide was so majestic, floating on top of the water like an anchored ship. I want the same for my castle.

The dead boy at my feet, I unroll the map. It gleams, ready for my voice. I speak clearly and with authority. It comes so naturally to me. "This kingdom will be called Emily—the rival of all!"

The word *Digglewip* appears across the top of the map. *What is the meaning of this?*

Again, I speak. "A grand hall for me to rule my subjects. I will be their king, and they will be my sheep."

Two structures appear on the map. My eyes shift to the sea. Nothing. But this is normal. Pippin arranged it all on the map before it manifested into reality.

But when I look again at the map, rage fills my veins. The two structures are none other than Pippin's Remembering Hall and Throne Room. *Relax. Relax, Michelle.* I breathe deeply. These only *resemble* the Brumbletide structures. They are not them. Continue.

"Towers for my endeavors," I command loudly now. "Towers for my endeavors and servant's quarters for my slaves! A dungeon for those who disobey me, and catacombs to throw away the remains of those who resist."

Thrill trimmers in my hands as I watch the Digglewip for my kingdom to appear. But where is it? Why is nothing happening? Shaking the map in frustration, I turn to the Snickerlings. "What's happened? Why is nothing appearing anymore?"

The magical creatures give no response, but their expressions are full of concern. They are rethinking their decision to follow me. This must be remedied quickly. When I turn to console them, my foot kicks the Snickerling boy, the source of what has been able to conjure thus far. It strikes me—he is not enough. *I need more.*

"Bring me more bodies! Now! As many as you can gather."

Breathtaking. The Snickerlings have chosen me as their master, so now they will do what I ask, even begrudgingly. This is undoubtedly a gift from the Universe. What else could it possibly be? Where or when has magic like this ever been found?

Hundreds of Snickerlings are brought for my cause. Pile upon pile of slain children stacked around. The Digglewip gleams brighter than it has since I've had it. It's working. *It's working!*

Then, almost at once, my kingdom blasts into existence on the map. Gleeful giggles escape me—I can't help it! It is beautiful. Glorious! *Perfect!*

The names Justice, Soleil, Michelle, Sara Lisa, George, Flori, and Eve appear on each of the seven towers. A frilly ferry bobs below in the Lux Sea.

Damn it all.

Chapter 10:
What of the Dragon?

I stare in horror. In utter disbelief. All of the bloodshed and battle that went into this moment—all to have *another Brumbletide?* The stag is more intelligent than I thought. He knew what he was doing, letting me go. Did he know what he was doing choosing me too? Certainly not.

What to do now? I have this sinking feeling that if I build this kingdom, the stag will be involved somehow. There must be a way to conquer it all. *Universe, Universe, what now?*

I look again at the kingdom on the Digglewip; not what I envisioned, but glorious, nonetheless. I look to the creatures who have willingly followed me. In the Snickerlings, I have not only servants but an army that will never die out as one appears in the place of the one that dies. A wealth of magic at my fingertips!

"Emily, rise!" I shout from the depths of my soul to the sea. I am both exhilarated and desperate.

Nothing—nothing at all.

But I have come this far, and I will not turn back. The Universe knows what I am—my destiny. The Universe is preparing me to be the ruler I am meant to be. The due diligence must be performed.

"Everyone, follow me. We must get to work."

Seven years. Seven years it took to get to where I am—seven long, tedious years. I have grown much as a ruler. Where before I had to fight my conscience at times, now it complies. So much blood from both human and creature has gone into the building of this palace. So much blood. The stag understands. So much blood is needed to build something of greatness. The traitors tried to rebel, of course, and not just the humans but Snickerlings as well. Thankfully, my loyal followers can keep them in line, and I've noticed the more of the original following that dies off, the ones born in their place are born loyal. This, I see, is a gift from the Universe.

The humans are by far the weakest link. They only build a little in a day, even with constant whippings. The only thing they will be useful for when all is finished is bringing the townspeople into the kingdom; even that, I am skeptical.

Something brings the reoccurring dream I used to have to mind. The Black Death delusion of me as king and my subjects adoring me as I walk to my throne. Who would have thought so much would go into making that scene reality? But I have built this kingdom with my bare hands. It was not handed to me. Greatness has a high cost. I have paid it and am willing to tithe to keep reaping its rewards.

Perhaps the highest cost was the sacrifice of the sorry sacks that gave me birth. The good memory of my parents walking with me is the only one of its kind. If there was ever anything I admired in Soleil, it was her ability to shrug off the horrors our father inflicted upon us. We were both subject to his unspeakable sins from my very earliest memory. Soleil managed to keep hope of a better life. Somehow, even *smile* during the hours of reprieve. But not I. Every time stuck to me like tar. Even if I managed to wash much of it away—which was almost never—there was still the sticky residue in my every pore. And its stickiness seemed to attract the vermin of the earth. Still, now, the residue remains like leprosy. There is no cure except greatness. The Universe has seen my anguish and heard my cries. It has accepted my dues paid and given me beauty for ashes. I am king of the greatest kingdom that will ever be. And it is almost time to fill it with souls.

"Pravius! Impius! Come!"

At once, my right-hand Snickerlings appear on the grassy knoll at the sea's edge where I supervise construction. They bow. "Yes, Sire."

"The palace is almost finished. The time has come to start persuading the people of Crescent and Fall to come."

"Wonderful, Sire, wonderful."

"You two have been loyal servants and have greatly aided in the creation of this magnificent kingdom. But unfortunately, the traitors will have to do this next job."

"Must they?" Impius whines.

"Yes. The townspeople are so far removed from Ipswich that they are no longer familiar with your kind. They will only respond to the humans."

"Sire, what you say is correct as always. May you grant a question?"

"I will."

"What of the Dragon?"

A heaviness drops in my gut. This has occurred to me several times through the years—the dragon in the room, if you will. Always lurking in the wings, the bridge that must be crossed one day soon or far. There has been no sign of him for seven years, and I had hoped that the Universe would have handled the situation before now.

The Dragon is the king of Crescent and Fall. It isn't likely that he will give up his subjects easily. As of now, I do not know how I will defeat him when the time arrives. Fear shrouds me, and I say a silent prayer to the Universe.

"If we may," offers Pravius, "we think you may want to go talk to the Dragon yourself."

"And say what?" I snap. "I am usurping your kingdom. I hope you don't mind."

The Snickerlings bow low. "O, King." *That never gets old.* "He has granted you to build this castle in the sea already. Couldn't he have done away with you by now if he wanted? We think Sire should go talk to him. Sire has a way with words. Look how you convinced so many to leave Pippin and follow you."

My face burns. "Gabriel!" Pravius and Impius fall to their faces, trembling. "How dare you mention that name to me. And how dare you say the Dragon has *granted* me anything!" Gabriel blows fire as he sits at my side like a good dog. A good dog the size of a small house. "Play with them, my pet."

Gabriel blasts fire from his snout at the children. They scream and fly away, Gabriel swiftly behind them, trying to catch them in his blazing streams.

I huff away my rage and ponder the words of the small boys. What will I do if the Dragon puts up a fight? How will I defeat the ancient demon who has ruled this land for centuries upon centuries?

Universe, help me. Grant me success in this impossible endeavor.

Brynn Miller, age 11

Brynn Miller, age 11

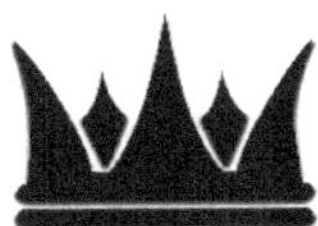

Chapter 11:
The Deal

I hated my mother. I hate even the memory of her now. I hate the way she spoke and laughed and ate. I hate the way she looked. I hated her weakness most. I am ashamed that I emerged from her body. How could I have come from something so unlike myself? Soleil is my mother. I am my father; whom I am ashamed to say I admire. He worked hard for his riches. We had money because he worked tirelessly, and that is admirable. Why have I never been able to put forth effort toward ordinary work the way he did? *Because I am meant for more.*

But while he gave us a wealthy life, he didn't love us. He saw Soleil and I as possessions to be used and put away at will. He never loved me, but if he knew the real me—what I am and my passions, he would have hated me as I hate him. If his ghost has been watching me, I can only imagine the horror in that misty face. I grin. "If you can hear me, I hate you."

From a young age, I have lived in secret, hiding my true passions and desires from a world that wouldn't understand. Alone, I have felt my feelings and explored my thoughts, and further and further away I grew from my family.

I hate Soleil. How dare she call me brother. Our only bond is blood—nothing else. She has no fathom of me. She has no idea what it's like to hide. She has no idea how monstrous life was for me and just how different we are.

No one will ever understand. No one will ever *try* to understand. And because so, I am left to myself, to fend for myself, to provide for myself, to love for myself, to learn and grow by myself. And the Universe has seen my suffering and has at last rewarded me.

In the cool of the day, I sit and watch as the finishing touches are put on my Emily. There is a rustling in the wood, and none other than the king of Crescent and Fall, the Dragon, appears. It is only he—no guards. The moment I have dreaded for seven years has finally arrived. I knew it would come eventually, and even though the Snickerlings warned me that they cannot kill him, I had fantasized that when he appeared, the Snickerlings would carry me to safety immediately. The Snickerlings working on the castle stop and see him, but he is far too close for them to save me now. "Your Majesty," I say to the Dragon with a bow. My skin crawls at addressing him this way.

"Rise. I will not hurt you," says the Dragon in the kindest manner yet with smoke billowing from his massive nostrils. He is hideous, yet his air commands respect somehow.

"I've been watching your construction here on my land—fine work, indeed."

He's been watching the whole time? I gulp. "Thank you, Sire." The weighty realization that I have not yet conquered everything sets in though I've known it in my heart for seven years. This land belongs to the Dragon, and I must somehow take it from his powerful clutches. *Do you hear me, Universe? If I've ever needed your help, I need it now!*

"As you know, this area is still under my dominion."

"Oh?"

The Dragon laughs hideously, amused at my feigned obliviousness. "I have a proposition for you, King Michelle."

King Michelle. He is mocking me. The hair rises on my neck. I will *not* be subject to him. He will not rule over me.

"I will give you this land peacefully."

There's a catch.

"If you allow me to mentor you in your building of this kingdom."

Universe? Is this you? There must be something in it for him.

"You're wondering what's in the deal for me."

My breath catches. *Can he read my thoughts?*

"You have already proven to be a worthy ruler. You stole servants and an army from under the nose of the great White Stag. And not only that, you have discovered the power that pours from the slain and have used it well."

I lift my chin.

"What harm would it bring to Crescent and Fall to be split into two great kingdoms? Why, this would be a wonderful thing, indeed. You can have this land. It will be yours alone if you allow me to show you how to use better the magic you have already discovered and extract even more from the creatures." His wing spreads toward the horde of Snickerlings flying around the castle. Many have stopped their work, curious as to what we are doing.

"Get back to work!" I shout.

Under the gaze of the Dragon, I ponder this proposition. It's too good to be true. Has the Universe blessed me again, or is this a trick? *Universe, if he is nefarious, protect me from his schemes.*

The Dragon sits back on his haunches and extends his great wings, making it appear that it is now only the two of us in a tent of meeting. He raises a claw. "Do we have a deal?"

Universe...

I ponder his proposition for a few moments but go with my gut in the end. I place my hand into the scaly claw, and the beast flashes his jagged teeth in a heinous grin.

"We have a deal," I reply.

THE DEAL

I will never call him Your Majesty again.

Chapter 12:
On the Other Side

"The power for you is in the tongue," says the Dragon.

"What do you mean for me?" I ask.

We are both watching the Snickerlings work away at Emily. It is an awe-inspiring spectacle, though identical to Brumbletide. In the end, it doesn't matter so much about the structure of the building—as long as it's glorious. I can add to the skeleton whatever I desire.

"You have discovered the power that is in the wings. You have used it well, though not to its full potential. But while the power from the wings gives magic *for* you, as seen in the creation of your castle here, the tongue gives magic *to* you." As he says this, before my very eyes, the Dragon transforms into a handsome young man.

"How did you do that?" I breathe.

The young man grins charmingly. "I told you. It is the power of the tongue. Silence the children, and unleash power you never fathomed possible."

I reach for the man's face to touch it, but just as I do, the Dragon appears again in a puff of smoke.

"Incredible," I say. "I will have the Snickerlings do this at once!"

"Oh, no, no, no."

"Why not?"

"*You* must do it."

Dread washes over me. I have not killed one Snickerling myself but only ordered my loyal servants to do it. The thought of harming one of the creatures myself sickens me.

The Dragon tilts its massive head. "What's wrong? Cat got your...tongue?" He grins like an idiot.

I scowl. "No. It's just that I haven't harmed the creatures with my own hand as of yet."

"Oh, yes, you have, my son. You masterfully lured them here to follow you instead of Pippin and then ordered the slaughtering of hundreds now. There is already much blood on your hands."

Just now, two Snickerlings fly to us and land with a bow. I stare, frozen, at the two of them—a boy and a girl. Strangely, when looking at the children, I am struck with memories of young Soleil and me.

"Master," says the boy. "I hate to inform you, but we have applied the last layer of paint on the drawbridge, and it is, in fact, red like Brumbletide Castle. We've tried everything. The paint only comes out red."

I hear nothing of his words but only stare at the boy in horror, trying to imagine how I would begin to kill him.

As if to know my thoughts—my inner soul—the Dragon speaks. "Greatness demands great sacrifice."

My head nods as if of its own will. "I can. I will."

"But will you do it *now*?"

I look alarmed at the Dragon. "Now?'

"Sire?" the Snickerling asks curiously.

"One moment," I snap at the boy. "I have no way of doing it right now."

"Behold." the Dragon swings its tail to me. Wrapped in it is an olive branch. I am shrouded with dread, knowing there is more than meets the eye to this olive branch.

"Call one," the Dragon says calmly.

My breath is a pant. I hold the gaze of the Dragon and hear myself say, "Boy, the paint is fine. Return. Girl, come to me."

I do not look as the boy flies away and the girl steps forward. I cannot bring myself to meet her eyes. The Dragon's grin brings me no peace.

"This is the price. On the other side, greatness waits. This is what will set you apart from all the kings of the earth. Take her hand."

Without thinking, I meet her eyes as I extend my hand to her. They are brown like that of a fawn, and watering. She knows.

As I grasp the small hand, the olive branch becomes a dagger. She doesn't scream or try to run. I think it might make it better if she did. But no, she submits to her fate because her kind are servants by nature.

"Your kingdom is at hand. Take it!"

Dear reader, I will spare you the explicit details of what happened next. But afterward, once that same old sadness came and went, I had no regrets.

Chapter 13:
Very Good

Stepping, stepping, stepping to my throne. Keep in time with the music, Michelle. Shoulders back, head high—the throne is much closer now. Cheers roar in the balconies.

"Michelle! Michelle! Long live Michelle!"

I reach my throne, the Throne of the Scepter. I turn, and the congregation applauds louder than ever. My lips part into a grin.

The Snickerlings amplify my voice through their mouths. My words boom throughout the Throne Room. "Thank you, my people. Please sit."

I watch the glimmering sea of crowns lower into the multitude of thrones throughout the balconies. My stomach wrenches at the sight as it has not ceased to do since this part of the scheme was enacted.

The traitors were ordered to go out into the town and tell the people of my new magnificent kingdom. They had one job—to bring the people! To persuade them to come to the castle and be a part of my kingdom through any means possible. But every one of the filthy traitors lied. Though I threatened them with their lives, they conspired together, and though they did go to the people, they told them not of my kingdom but of the stag's! Of how they could come and be a royal and rule a kingdom of their very own!

People started coming. They were coming in droves. I killed the first few for the abomination they spewed until it became evident that *all* the people coming from the town were told the same thing—all of them in sheer glee over the concept.

Appalled, I consulted the Dragon. I required his expertise since not only were there now masses of idiots waiting to be kings and queens, but the traitors escaped! Though I sent them out surrounded by Snickerling guards, they managed to escape. The Snickerlings lied to me and said it was the stag that did it. He is dead. And now, so are the Snickerlings who failed their task. The magic from their wings and tongues pulse through me as I remember their slaying.

The Dragon advised me to do something that at first seemed counterproductive. He said to *continue on with* this ridiculous idea of the people being Emily royals.

"Absolutely not."

"Absolutely yes, Michelle."

"How in the name would that ever benefit me? Not only would Emily then be the stag's kingdom, but also full of *actual* royals themselves! No, I will not entertain this ridiculous plan."

"Michelle."

King Michelle.

"Michelle, this is what you want. As long as they think they are royals, you've got them in the palm of your hand. Trust me, son. I've been in this business for many centuries." Smoke billows from his nostrils. "The smaller the distance between your path and Pippin's, the greater the deception, my friend. A path so close to the truth is much easier taken."

The truth? How dare he? Nonesense. Emily is my truth! I ponder his words while watching the continued work on my Emily. Its great towers are a marvel to behold. What the Dragon is saying makes sense, I hate to say. But how will I pull it all off? Can I pull it off?

"You have me on your side, my son, and the Universe has already shown you favor." He says this as if it were a very common thing for the Universe to show favor. I grunt.

Still ruminating in rebellious thoughts toward the Dragon, I fix my gaze on Emily and again plunge into fantasy...

Multitudes. Multitudes of royally adorned commoners fill the Throne Room, cheering on their king. They are loyal to him and will do anything he asks; they give him all they have because he has dressed them up in a gown and crown and let them have tea in his castle from time to time. It occurs to me how jealous all the other kings of the world will be that even my subjects look so splendid.

"Michelle! Michelle! Long live Michelle!"

There is no sign of the stag, only their true king, King Michelle the Immortal, who will rule them with an iron fist for all eternity. Generation upon generation will come, serve me, and go, but I will last and reign through them all. I will be the literal life of the people.

"Long live Michelle," I whisper and realize I said this aloud.

The Dragon flashes his fangs. "Good. Very good."

Chapter 14:
Sorcerer

"Death to the king! Death to the king!" they chant. The chants from the town are so loud I hear them from my throne. The people of Crescent and Fall are rising against me. After bringing so much beauty and meaning to their pathetic little lives, this is the thanks I get.

I am now one hundred and thirty-two years old, according to Crescent and Fall. Little do they know that I am actually two hundred or so. Time did not pass the same way in Brumbletide that it does in the real world. While it seemed I was only there a short time, I began to notice that the way people lived outside the Axiom was different than before I went in. When I went to retrieve our family servant from the Everly estate, it was not only empty, but someone had buried the servant in the yard. What an abhorrence. I would have never allowed a servant to be buried on the grounds. But it was by this and other revelations I knew it had been around a century that I was gone. I have ruled Emily and brought a great congregation to my kingdom. Multitudes.

The Dragon was right. The people are vain imbeciles. When I offered them even the façade of royalty, they came running like rats to cheese and worshiped me in gratitude as I snapped their tales in my trap.

But now, they have forgotten it all—all of the miracles done before their very eyes, all of the riches they basked in when in my Emily. They have forgotten every blessing bestowed upon them because not a single hair on my head has gone grey. Not an inch of my skin has wrinkled. My back has not hunched. I have not aged a day since the stag gave me the stone of eternity. I am now one hundred and thirty-two years old but look every bit a young man. And now, the wretched people of this town, the ungrateful dolts who deserve to die in their swill, have the nerve to shout, "Sorcerer!" and demand my dethroning.

Who will dethrone me? This is all mine. I have the power to kill them all, and now it appears that is the only way. Anyone not for me is against me. I rise, summoning the power of the tongue. I feel the surge of energy run through me, pulsing toward my crown. With each step, it grows stronger. My hatred fuels it. I'll kill them all.

But on my way to the castle's front balcony, a breath of fire knocks me to the ground. I roll to the edge of the stairs, almost falling down them. The Dragon sits in my Throne Room like a great gargoyle with his webby wings spread.

"How dare you! What are you doing?" I yell.

"Keeping you from doing something you will regret."

"They've all turned. They say, 'Death to the king.' They must die."

"They only need to see things in a different light." He vanishes and becomes the handsome young man again.

Still sprawled on the ground, I ask. "Is that how Crescent and Fall sees you?"

In a puff, he is back to his hideous self. "No. They see me as I am. Old sorcery is much easier to accept."

"Death to the king! Death to the king!" I clap my hands over my ears as the voices shriek and echo through the Throne Room. A bolt of fire streams to my feet, and I scream and curl them into my chest. "Stop that!"

"Rise, fool. Act like a king!"

I stand.

"You have the power to remedy this." He stretches his wing to the swarm of Snickerlings overhead.

"I've extracted so much already."

"If you intend to reign for a while, you must extract continually."

The dread sinks in like lead. Even all these years later, the dread still weighs heavy.

"Choose another. I will show you."

Overhead, the Snickerling creatures are glorious as always. The people love them; they are the main attraction of the castle. Little do they know, the Snickerlings *are* the magic of the castle in more ways than one.

"You there, boy! Come here!" I call.

The boy, so small and plain for such a magnificent creature, flies down to me and bows with his thumbs in his suspenders. He trembles at the Dragon. I take him by the hand without looking into his eyes, and the Dragon and I lead him to the catacombs.

That day, the Dragon showed me what becomes of one who drinks the blood of the slain. And that day, the people of Crescent and Fall received a new king.

Chapter 15:
Long Live the Firebreather

In the catacombs, we took the life, and we—I—did the unspeakable act of drinking the blood of the magical creature. Reader, I know you think you would never lower yourself to such depths, but you would. We think we know ourselves. We think we are good. We think our hearts will lead us to the right path. When, in fact, there is no "good." There is only "right." And the more you live, the more you learn that everyone has their own "right." Indeed, we think we know ourselves, but we do not until the time arrives to awaken new "wicked" pieces of you that have been there the whole time.

Dear reader, the feeling. The sheer ecstasy that flooded me that night. No words can describe it adequately as if every nerve in me was a ruler itself. The memory is still so vivid. And then the Dragon spoke.

"What do you want to become now? Anything. Anyone."

I close my eyes. The best moment of my life. As if every good feeling I have ever felt are all happening at once. As if on cue, my idea of the perfect man conjures in my mind. He is tall and brawny with wide bone structure. A strong chin is under a handsome beard matching a full head of waving chestnut hair—the eyes sparkling amber.

I'm growing. As I see him in my mind, I feel my shoulders broaden, and my hands become larger and stronger. I place them on my full beard and then run them through my thick locks. I caress the firm and broad face of the magnificent specimen.

The Dragon smiles proudly. "A beauty. What will you name him?"

I've kept a name in store for if I ever had a son, though I knew I never would.

"Thornus. His name is Thornus."

"Has a nice ring. Now, get some rest. Tomorrow, your people will meet their new king."

Laying in my canopy as my new self, I cannot sleep. The possibilities are endless with this new magic that has been bestowed upon me. Never in my wildest dreams could I have imagined all of this happening the way it has. It is otherworldly. The Universe has risen me to power using its hidden jewels reserved for those chosen to lead the masses.

"Universe, I will not fail you."

This morning, a letter went out to all the people of Crescent and Fall that there was to be a Changing of the Crowns this very night. Multitudes gather in the Throne Room to see it. King Michelle was in good health. Had their complaint been listened to and a new king found and brought to the throne? Who is he?

Fools.

I am in my chambers, listening to the song of the Snickerlings and admiring King Thornus in the levitating mirror. My crown sits on my gorgeous head, and I place the onyx at the top. My crown has six points, four of which are stars, and two are stones—my onyx, which I frequently remove to keep on my person, and Soleil's white onyx. Why do I not have all of the stones of the Chosen on my crown, you ask? Because no matter what I do, they disappear into the Resplendent. I have locked them away, buried them, and thrown them into the sea, yet they always come back to The Resplendent. I know it is impossible, but I cannot shake the feeling that it might be the ghost of the stag.

As always, the crown becomes part of me when I wear it. Even if I were to have the strongest man in the land pull with all his might, it would not leave my head until I asked it to come off— and kindly. Another lesson from the Dragon. He really has been quite helpful. The crown has always stayed on because of the stones, but now, with the blood of the Snickerlings in my veins, a synergy exists—I am one with the crown, the stone, and their power.

The Snickerling's song quiets, and trumpets blast. My silly royally dressed King's Hand announces me.

"Kings and Queens, Princes and Princesses of Emily! Townspeople of Crescent and Fall with a royal destiny, please rise! We gather here today for a Changing of the Crowns. Our beloved King Michelle the Immortal, the greatest king that ever lived of the greatest kingdom there ever was, has at last been laid to rest after a long, healthy reign as Head King of Emily. Though many of you were ungrateful and called for his removal and should be put to death for your foolishness."

The room is uncomfortably silent. Fools. Ungrateful fools.

The King's Hand continues. "But now, a new day dawns. New blood takes the Head Throne tonight! Ladies and gentlemen, I present to you, your king—"

"Pippin!" a voice in the congregation shouts.

My legs almost buckle. What did they say?

The King's Hand pauses, obviously taken aback at the audacity.

The voice dares to speak again. "Pippin, the great White Stag, is the one true king!"

Another voice. "Pippin's everywhere around this castle. You can't get away from him! You will never compete!"

My skin goes clammy. That statement was for me; I know it. I charge out of my chambers, down the hall, and peek from behind the curtain into the Throne Room. Hooded figures speckle the congregation—the traitors, certainly!

"Pippin is the real king and is the only reason any other king exists! He rules now in Brumbletide and will redeem even this abomination!"

A woman's voice. "Long live King Pippin! Long live King Pippin!"

And the flock of sheep that is the congregation joins in! Imbeciles! They don't even know him. If only this castle didn't have the stag's hoofprints all over it. This is *my castle—my kingdom!*

I breeze into the Throne Room as cheers roar, but I know that they are still cheering over the stag and not me.

The King's Hand looks at me helplessly and yells in defiance. "Crescent and Fall! *SILENCE! This* is your new king! King Thornus of Firebreather!"

The cheers continue. The most unsatisfactory reception because it is impossible to know who it is for. The hooded figures are gone. I must hunt them and kill them as my first line of work as King Thornus.

Snickerlings guide me to the Throne of the Scepter. The King's Hand quiets the crowd so that I can address them. It takes all the patience I can muster to be calm and collected during my speech. What a bunch of senseless buffoons.

I beam. "Friends, royals, your majesties, lend me your ears. It is with utmost pleasure that I take the Head Throne as your Head King of Emily. This kingdom is the most miraculous and magical in all the world." I lift my hands to the Snickerlings swarming and warmouths darting here and there. "And I cannot help but suspect that each of you has been chosen by the Powers That Be to be a special part of it."

"That power is Pippin! And the true kingdom is Brumbeltide!" yells a voice.

I swallow but do not flinch. I shift my eyes over the congregation. Where did the voice come from?

"I am honored to serve as your Head King. The line of Firebreather has been chosen to rule, and as I am my Uncle Michelle's next of kin, this privilege is in my hands. To Michelle be the glory and dominion—"

"To Pippin be the glory and dominion!" shouts the voice.

I grind my teeth and squeeze my hands into fists but continue. "For king and country, my people." I force through clenched teeth.

As I fight to finish my address, from above us all, out of thin air, fall thousands of little red biscuits. They fall all around the Throne Room and into everyone's hands. They fall onto the thrones and on the floor. The Throne Room is covered with the strange biscuits. The people shout in glee at the magical happening. Murmurs and whispers are heard of messages hidden inside.

One falls at my feet, and I pick it up to examine it. A curious biscuit indeed; a type of fur covers it. I break it open, and indeed, there is a tiny scroll inside.

Your lie will lead many to the truth.

I drop the biscuit and step on it as if it has burst into flames. I storm off to my chambers.

"Your majesties, your new king, King Thornus the Firebreather!" calls the King's Hand desperately.

A smattering of distracted, tepid cheers come from the people who are still opening the biscuits and reading the messages inside. Squeals of delight and curious murmurs speckle the applause.

"Stupid sheep," I mutter as I open the door to my chambers. "True sheep. Stupid as the day is long."

I remove my robe and look into the mirror, levitating before me. The magic of this castle! It is incredible and all because of me. These idiots have no idea what surrounds them.

My reflection strikes me. I am a stallion. My beauty is exquisite. I touch my face and smile at myself. I could look all day.

The people *will* love me. I will win them. I wink at the beautiful specimen that gazes dreamily back at me.

Oh, yes, they won't know what hit them.

Chapter 16:
A Sophisticated Plan

Thornus the Beautiful reigned for one hundred years. Each Head of Castle lived longer than average but not too long to where they would be suspected a sorcerer. In Emily's history books, it is printed that the people unjustly killed King Michelle after accusing him of sorcery, and he died of a broken heart.

I wasn't able to change the books in the library until the third Head of Castle—me again—took the throne. Until then, the library, Michelle Tower, was my office and kept off-limits to the public. But with blood, much blood, I was able to pull off the one enchantment I am most proud of to this day.

Thornus was a beautiful king, and the people loved him—they loved me. But it was as Thornus that I worked closely with the Dragon to orchestrate the most sophisticated deception no one has ever known. We spun every one of our tales from one origin—Pippin. Disgustingly, when Pippin's name is used, the people will do whatever is asked without even a hint of a fight. We even built Emily's systems from bits and pieces of Pippin's methods—just enough to draw the sheep in, to enchant them, to woo them, and then have them for good.

We lifted the subjects out of their poverty for a moment—just a moment—while they were in Emily. For the few hours they were in the castle, they were shown the royal treatment complete with titles, respect, thrones, feasts, and the chance to even look like a royal for a cost. This, the buying of the costume, separated the Haves from the Have-nots. One of the most critical parts of this sophisticated plan is always to ensure that Haves and Have-nots remain. It is crucial to ensure this so that there is a never-ending cycle of Haves being watched by Have-nots who have no chance in the world of ever becoming a Have but hoping and believing in anything that might give them the chance of becoming a Have. But let us not forget the ever-important Have-somes. These desire to be Haves just as much as the Have-nots but will give all they have to *appear* at least to be a Have. This fools both the Have-nots *and* the Have-somes themselves! The Have-nots watch the Have-somes and begin to believe there is hope for themselves. And the Have-somes, after spending themselves into a pit, do not see the pit but only see the adoration of the Have-nots and begin to believe that they have, in fact, become Haves.

The sale of the palace garments ensured the above was a well-oiled machine. But for those who could not afford to purchase a gown and crown, just being referred to as "Your Majesty" and being bowed to by the Snickerlings was enough to gain not only their loyalty but also their worship.

They loved me, the only one to have ever blessed them with a short reprieve from their pathetic, miserable lives. They came in droves. They brought their children, they trained them in the ways of Emily, and I and the Dragon were there to help them every step of the way.

By my third incarnation, a queen named Delores the Shrewd—I had always been fond of that name for a girl—the Dragon and I devoted the many corridors of the castle to dormitories for an academy to breed total indoctrination of their children. After only a few generations of people who were ecstatic to have their children attend the magical academy that was like none other in the world, Emily was engrained not only into Crescent and Fall but into the very fabric of the families and passed down to the next generations like an heirloom.

Emily became more and more renowned. Not only was it the most powerful castle in all the world, but it was now the richest. Each Head of Castle was more beloved and more renowned than the last. King Michelle was known to be the founder, the builder, the best and brightest of Pippin's Chosen Seven—Pippin's right-hand man. Any accusation of sorcery was gone because of the history books in the library. The library was an incredibly elaborate undertaking that has reaped generations of spoils. The blood, the magical blood of the Snickerlings, had to be not only diluted but *ingested* by the people of Crescent and Fall. Diluted so they would not become themselves powerful like me but ingested so that they would see what I wanted them to see.

Like poison given in small amounts to cause immunity, the Snickerling blood was diluted and given to the people to eat in their delicacies of the feasts at Batch. The books have not changed, but the way people see them has. Although, through the generations, Emily has had such influence that now even people who have never been to the castle see history in a whole new way. Now, even I only see the books in the proper light. My light.

The Snickerling Massacre of Delores had only to happen once. The people have passed the enchantment down through their bodies, and it even resides in the air. Once someone joins the academy and has been through a fitting, they see as we see.

This all worked splendidly for three solid generations before there was any hiccup.

Chapter 17:
Rise and Fall

Three magnificent rulers for over three hundred years. Emily rose to unprecedented heights. Whether they believed it or not, much of the world had heard of Emily's unimaginable magic and riches, and many came from great distances to see it.

The only thing that decreased was the warmouths. Unfortunately, when they died, a new one did not appear in their place like the Snickerlings. This unfortunate detail was unbeknownst to me when I slaughtered a mass of them at once for a project in Germany.

So it was by the end of Delores's reign, the castle was functioning at peak performance. The catacombs hummed with glowing wings, the castle and The Resplendent were thoroughly infused with Snickerling magic. When a new student came to the castle and went through a fitting, we had them, and so much so that any descendent who came after them would be drawn in immediately as well. The magic that binds their crown traveled to each descendent, calling them to their destiny as an Emily royal.

Even the fire in every fireplace, on every candle wick, and every torchless flame lighting the corridors worked together for me. It miraculously doesn't burn the skin—the people love it—but it speaks to me at night about what the people are saying in the castle. The voice—it is so familiar.

I was king of the world, and I could have taken it as my own except for the discrepancy that arose during the final years of Delores the Shrewd. A plain, meek student, completely unassuming, came to the palace. Her parents had never been to the castle, which should have told me something the minute I heard. They enrolled their daughter, Gemma was her name, into the academy. Of course, I didn't see them. I had many servants working for me at that point. She was enrolled, and then at her fitting, she received none other than Eve's crown! Until then, I had no idea the crowns of the Chosen were in Emily! To this day, I am not sure if they are the actual crowns of the Chosen, but the crown the girl wore held Eve's lapis lazuli. The ghost of the stag—that was the only explanation unless I had a traitor in my midst. But why would they only take the stones to The Resplendent time after time? And why on earth would the ghost of Pippin keep putting them there?

None of it makes any sense. I fear that it is, in fact, the ghost of the stag. He toys with me for no other reason than torment. Every so often, when I think I am free of him, he drops more of his nonsense here, which the stupid people always adore, and no matter what the Dragon and I do, whatever he leaves is stuck here, indestructible. Even my secret entrance to the dungeon now has a hideous statue of the stag over it! He taunts me to drive me mad. But he underestimates my desire to be great. Madness fuels me.

The girl. At first, nothing seemed to be a problem. She was placed in Firebreather House so we could keep watch. But her arrival happened during the perfect storm. The end of Delores was close, so I was preparing for my next metamorphosis. This time, I was going for a wiser and more distinguished look: a tall, willowy king named Lorenzo. I spent many hours in the catacombs with the Snickerlings. The change was more difficult this time because the Dragon had left me on my own. It was time.

While I was deep in the works, the girl weaseled her way into the people's hearts. Even with all the magic oozing out of every one of Emily's pores, the people, the students, the Queen Mothers even—all fools—loved her! And our plan of placing her in Firebreather House backfired. Everyone, every "royal" idiot in the palace and in the town, petitioned for her to be the next Head of Castle—she was a Firebreather, after all. I learned many things in that era, many things. But much would be set backward in the learning of those lessons.

Still Delores, I paced in my chambers.

"Dragon!" I call into the air. He appeared at once.

"Yes, my Queen."

"Very funny," I retort. "The people have petitioned for Gemma Zechariah to be Head of Castle! What do I do? I told you we shouldn't let them think they were royal in any way. What if they rise in revolt against me when they don't get her as a queen?"

The Dragon sits calmly as I pace. "You could kill them all."

I stop, pondering the repercussions.

"But every tyrant meets his end quickly," he adds.

Huffing, I return to my pacing.

"I say you let her rise."

I gasp.

"And then kill her shortly after," the Dragon says nonchalantly.

"I refuse to give the Head Throne to another."

"Then do what you think necessary. You are the greatest king in history. You will figure it out."

"I don't know what to do."

"Calm down. She's just a girl."

"She wears Eve's crown. She is not just a girl. The ghost of Pippin is up to something again. He taunts me so."

"The ghost of Pippin? Is that what you've been calling him?"

"What else would he be?"

"Son, the Stag is not dead."

My mouth falls open, and I swallow a lump. "Pippin is dead. I killed him." Even as the words leave my mouth, I know they aren't true. I've known all these years but couldn't bring myself to face it.

"The Stag lives and is more powerful than you and I. He allows all of this."

I squint in disbelief. "That is a lie. He would never allow me to do all of this."

"Believe what you like, but he could wipe all of this out at any point. He could take all of the stones of the Chosen back. He could take over this kingdom anytime, and you could do nothing about it."

"LIAR!" I yell. My blood boils. "That is a lie! Leave me! I'll do all this myself."

The Dragon watches me calmly. He is always calm. "As you wish. But at the end of the day, all of this is gaining you slaves for a while. One day, you will be a slave with them. It is the fate of us all who have chosen this path." And with that, he disappears.

He is a liar. I tell myself. He has grown jealous of all he has helped accomplish and is now lying to me to keep me from continuing in greatness. I am on my own now. But the Universe has prepared me well; this girl is only a test to pass.

"I'll kill her now," I say to Delores in the mirror.

In the middle of the night, I slip on my hooded cloak and silently slink to Firebreather Hall. I must be as quiet and stealthful as possible because of the dormmate. If necessary, I will kill her too, though I hate the thought of killing a Firebreather. I think of them as part of Emily, like the walls and windows. Silently, so smoothly, I push open the heavy scarlet, oak door where *Princess Coraline Ravenwood, Daughter of Michelle* and *Princess Gemma Zechariah, Daughter of Eve* are lit magically in gold. The room is still and quiet; no movement comes from either canopy bed except for the heavy breathing of slumber. It brings me comfort to hear, and I breeze into the room and to the bed of Eve's descendant. She sleeps peacefully. I haven't slept like that in centuries. I crouch beside her and, with a swift move, touch my crown and blast a beam of silver light directly at her chest. It rises and falls, rises and falls, rises and falls... then no more. But the dormmate sits up. She has heard me. I immediately roll underneath Gemma's bed, hiding behind the purple velvet drapery. I see the bare feet of the dormmate step hastily to Gemma. She shakes her. No gasp, no scream—a true Firebreather—but she does run. I watch her feet as she opens the dormitory door and runs to the right down the corridor. I quickly roll from under the bed and hasten out behind her but to the left, back to my chambers through a secret passageway behind a large portrait of a flying serpent. I remove my cloak and get into bed. Not two minutes later, there is a commotion and then a knock at my door. I groggily get back out of bed and open it to two concerned-looking Snickerlings, a boy and a girl.

"What is it? What brings you here to disturb me at this ungodly hour?"

"Queen Delores, there has been a death in Firebreather Hall. The students are gathered at the dormitory of young Princess Gemma."

"Why do you continue to refer to them in that silly way?"

The two Snickerlings bow low. "Apologies, Your Majesty. We thought you would want to know."

"Of course, I want to know. I want to know all that happens in my palace. Just a minute." I grab Delores's tiara and follow the Snickerlings to Firebreather Hall.

The corridor is crowded with sniffling, tear-stained students gathered at the door I just left.

"What has happened?" I ask.

A Bravetail girl chokes, "It—it's Gemma, Your Majesty. She's—she's dead!" She and many other students burst into sobs.

But just as I straighten my shoulders to handle my task, an Ironsnout boy gasps. "Look! Look, everyone! She's breathing. Gemma's breathing!"

Panic sweeps me. I shove through the students into the dormitory. Gemma, who lay splayed across her bed, is, in fact, breathing! The Queen Mothers make their way through the crowd and come up behind me. The Queen Mother of Justice Tower makes it into the room first.

"Queen Mother Madeline," pipes the Ironsnout boy. "Gemma died in the night. But now she has come back to life!"

Queen Mother Madeline watches the girl curiously. Under our gaze, Gemma blinks open her eyes and sits up. She looks overjoyed that everyone is in her room. "Why, what is this? What are you all doing here?" She smiles.

"Gemma!" pipes the Bravetail running to embrace her. "You died in the night, but now you are alive!" Gemma is taken aback but places her arms around the Bravetail. I watch the whole scene in disbelief.

The Queen Mother of the Hanging Gardens says, "This is a sign. We knew it before, but now it is certain. Gemma is to be the next Head of Castle Emily!"

"Yes!" yells the Bravetail. "Yes! Long live Queen Gemma! Long live Queen Gemma!" And all the students and Queen Mothers join in.

Gemma looks at me empathetically as if aware that this may offend me and wants no part of it. It takes all I have, but I manage a smile at the stupid girl. I step to her side. I have no choice but to act on the Dragon's suggestion. "We are relieved that you are alright, Princess. And it looks like you have quite the future ahead of you." I indicate the crowd of chanting children and Queen Mothers. Even some Snickerlings have joined in!

"I—I don't know what to say," Gemma replies humbly.

I place my hand on the girl's back. It is soft—a knife will go in easily. "Say 'yes' for starters."

She laughs joyfully and, after a moment of hesitation, says, "I would be honored," to the crowd that goes wild.

She and I exchange an amused glance. An understanding that I will help her rise to take my place on the Head Throne.

I will make her rise. Then I will kill her and make sure she stays dead forever.

Chapter 18:
Queen Gemma the Extraordinary

And so, the grooming and training up of Gemma to be the next Head Queen began. She and I worked side-by-side as I taught her the ways of a queen. The posture, the poise, the air, the command of respect, yet the manipulation of the masses to gain their loyalty. She listened and learned intently.

What I did not see coming was that I would *enjoy* our time together. Gemma is every bit a true queen. Wise, brilliant, hardworking, and poised, yet nonchalant when necessary. Her demeanor commands a crowd, and they only want more of her. I found myself taking pride in her as my pupil.

But greatness—true greatness—begs of these moments that you act according to plan no matter what your feelings beg of you.

She must die. And she will die by my hand.

Toward the end of January, I knew the time for a Changing of the Crowns had come. We had just celebrated Cervi Day, a beastly event that has had to happen ever since the very first December in the castle. I was still in my original form, Michelle the Immortal, when suddenly, one day, it was snowing *inside* Emily! A strange happening, and it wasn't all. Glitter and bauble-filled garland had somehow decorated every tower, turret, banister, and eave. Festive decor was everywhere inside and outside, like a horde of Christmas spirits vomited all over my castle in the night. A tree! A gargantuan tree sat like a giant ogre on my floor, reaching almost to the ceiling. And worst of all, purple draperies hung from every balcony in the Throne Roam with the head of the stag on every single one! I feared greatly that Emily and I were done for. The Dragon was right that the stag had somehow come back to life and was here for a reckoning. But nothing happened. Though I spent it in anxious sweat, the day was lovely, and the townspeople fell in love with Emily all the more. A day like it has happened once every December since—another taunt from the ghost of the stag that I have yet again managed to work into my scheme.

So, as my century as Delores the Shrewd comes to a close, January is a good time to make the switch while the people are still in merry moods from the last Cervi Day.

The Snickerlings bring Gemma to my chambers at my command. She steps in solemnly and curtsies to me as I lay in my grand canopy.

"You summoned me, my Queen?"

"Yes, Gemma. The time has come for you to rule in my place." As the words leave my lips, I seethe, even knowing my plan.

"Oh dear, no, Your Majesty! You still have time. Plenty of time!" Her eyes well, and her voice cracks. She truly adores me. "My heart breaks at the thought of you leaving me," her big brown doe eyes sparkle with tears. A glint of something I have never felt before stabs at my conscience, and I have to push it away into the dark space of my brain, where I keep the sadness.

A feeble cough. "I am afraid I don't have much time, my dear. The letters have gone out announcing to Crescent and Fall that there will be a Changing of the Crowns ceremony tomorrow night. You must be ready."

"Tomorrow night?" she breathes. "That is so sudden!" A tear falls down her cheek. The girl really is quite emotional. She throws her arms around my neck. How dare she touch me. I pat her on the back gently. "There, there, child. It is time. Snickerlings, bathe and groom Gemma for the event."

"Yes, Your Majesty." Gemma boards the white carpet that the Snickerlings hold for her. "I owe so much to you, my Queen. I am forever grateful." She wipes her tears and waves goodbye as she is flown out of my chambers to The Respendent.

The trumpets sound. I sit on my throne, repulsed by the masses here to see Gemma become queen. Never in all my time in Emily have so many "royals" *and* townspeople gathered in this throne room for anything.

I did not walk to my throne. The Snickerlings brought me by carpet and set me on it, considering "my condition." I am supposedly too old to walk any distance by myself. My crown sits on my head, but the onyx is on a necklace around my neck. A few times now, I have forgotten that it is, in fact, the onyx that has kept me alive for hundreds of years now and have let go of it. Horrors ensued as I came too near to death for comfort. Now, it is second nature to always keep it on me.

Tonight, Gemma will be crowned with Justice's crown. Justice! She is a descendant of the drunk as well! I was utterly speechless when we found out during her fitting for Head Queen—squeals of delight from the Queen Mothers and Snickerlings. The Snickerlings continue to make me question their loyalty. But the drunk's crown—how it made its way to her, I still do not know. I suspect the stag. He plays with me. I hate him with my whole being.

The Snickerling's song quiets, and a boy hovers in the midst of the Throne Room. That one is Asher. I remember the face.

"Hear ye! Hear ye! Welcome one, welcome all to the ever-prestigious Changing of the Crowns ceremony! Today, Queen Delores the Shrewd will crown the next Head of Emily Castle. Everyone, please rise and acknowledge Her Royal Majesty, Queen Delores!"

The balconies erupt with applause. I wave my hand in thanks to my congregation.

"And now, for the next to take the Throne of the Scepter. Everyone, turn your gaze to the lovely Princess Gemma of Firebreather House!"

The congregation loses their minds with cheers and roars as I grind my teeth.

Gemma breezes into the Throne Room dressed in a beautiful emerald green gown. She smiles and waves joyfully at everyone as if they were all long-lost friends. Everything I have taught her about poise and elegance goes out the window as she gushes to the audience.

She has made it to the Throne of the Scepter, and I force a smile. The Snickerlings that carry the train of her gown are absolutely gleeful. I want to vomit, but I clench my teeth and take her hands when she comes to me and kisses my cheeks.

The Snickerling, Asher, yells, "I present to you your new Head of Castle, Queen Gemma of Firebreather!" The crowd roars so loudly my skin turns cold with bumps.

"And now, our beloved Queen Delores will crown Queen Gemma."

The room falls silent to watch me give away my throne. I do not rise. I make Gemma come to me. Everyone understands because I am supposedly on death's door, but truth be told, I refuse to stand for her.

Justice's crown is beside me on a red pillow. I take it up, and Gemma leans down. I could easily kill her right now.

I set Justice's crown on her head and immediately see the change in her eyes as she feels the surge of power that only the crowns holding the stones of the Chosen release. She breathes deeply, stands, and faces the people who yell with adoration for her. Gemma plants kisses in her hands and throws them to her people—*my people.*

A man's throaty voice yells louder than all the others. His words are clear. "Long live Queen Gemma the Extraordinary!" And the whole congregation begins to chant, "Long live Queen Gemma the Extraordinary! Long live Queen Gemma the Extraordinary!"

Extraordinary? How in the world would they know? She just became Head Queen; she's done nothing so far. What stupid people.

But now, the time has come to execute my plan.

The gleeful chants turn into gasps of horror as Queen Delores the Shrewd falls dead on the floor.

Chapter 19:

Gemma

It was the end of January. Yes, the twenty-seventh, when I, Gemma, shockingly took the Head Throne of Emily. It has all been a whirlwind—all ten years.

I am the only child of my beloved parents. The three of us lived together in a small cottage in the woods of the In Between. It happened one day when we were in town, we went by the bakery. I had two little friends I enjoyed seeing when we were in town: the baker's daughter, Martha, and the bartender's son, Gus. They were both younger than me but so much fun. The three of us would laugh together while our parents talked about grown-up things. This is exactly what we were doing that day, but this time, our parents were speaking privately in the bakery. That was the last time I saw Martha and Gus for a long while. I miss those two so much.

After that meeting in town, my mother and father told me I would be enrolled in the academy of Emily Castle. I couldn't have been more surprised by the news. We were a poor family; we didn't belong in the castle, let alone Emily Academy, but they both spoke of Pippin the White Stag and the Chosen and all of these things they had never spoken of before. So, I came here to the castle. And dear reader, the palace, I can't describe it adequately. Glorious! Not only the exquisite beauty of the castle you imagine in your dreams with its massive painted windows, murals on the ceilings, and endless corridors and stairwells—you never knew what you'd find in them! The magical creatures! Beautiful, sweet little flying children called Snickerlings and flying animals called warmouths. The Snickerlings would sing the most breathtaking songs that were tailored magically to what *you* wanted to hear. The most pristine little children, so small yet so miraculous. Bless their hearts. They cater to every whim of the castle royals. The animals, much rarer than the Snickerlings, were no less miraculous, so it was extra special when you happened upon one. An owl named Felixus took a liking to me and has been invaluable to me in my time here.

I came to this castle a naïve girl of thirteen, awestricken by the magical happenings of Emily, and I hadn't even yet experienced the miraculous seven towers. But it was when I went to my fitting in The Resplendent that everything took a turn. I gleefully received a beautiful gown that fitted itself to my body. I watched, mouth agape, as glass slippers formed perfectly to my feet. My eyes grew wider and wider as I watched the Snickerling brush my tangled, mousy brown hair into a silky mane of luxurious locks. But then, it was time to receive my crown. It was a strange experience trying on crowns of every shape, size, and color and then trying everything possible to get them to fall off. Of course, most did, but after many colorful hatboxes had been opened, what was the crown that chose me? None other than that of Queen Eve of the Chosen!

Everyone was shocked, not at all least of them, myself. The crown, dear reader, again, the words evade me. The crown, *it becomes* something when I wear it. *I become* something when I wear it. I feel different—alive—and like the crown is somehow alive. I still wonder to this day if it is. I had to promise to come back to it in order to take it off. It wouldn't allow me to part with it without a promise that I would return.

After that, though I wore the crown of Eve of Ironsnout, I was placed in Firebreather Hall with Bastille Anguis as my dormmate. She was a quiet girl with a very solemn disposition. She wasn't harsh, but she wasn't kind either.

The classes, the classes! I will never forget them as long as I live—which won't be much longer. My first Emily class was in the glorious Hanging Gardens of Flori. Dear reader, again I cannot describe them adequately. First, the way into the tower was through the trunk of the most beautiful and mystical wisteria tree. Once through it, we were in another world. It had to be another world, another realm. There is no way this colossal and extraordinary garden could be in the tower we saw from the outside! To look at the tower from the ferry's dock, the size of it doesn't match up. The tree is a portal to another world. It has to be.

Justice Tower, where we learned Hospitality, was a castle itself. A castle inside a castle. Also, in this tower, we learned how to address our subjects in a class called Subjects. Of all the classes, I was drawn to and excelled in Hospitality/Subjects most. I loved caring for others. They were always grateful, but it was me that was the most grateful. It brought me pure joy to serve and help the royals of Emily. I have made many friends in Hospitality, but I loved almost everyone I have met here—wonderful, wonderful souls.

I surprised myself in Hoplology. Handling the heavy, strange, and sometimes alarming weapons came naturally to me, and I even enjoyed it. We learned a game—dear reader, a death-defying game called Gottfrig's Grab. It is utterly terrifying but loads of fun. You catch your opponent in a net, but both of you must keep from falling into a blazing fire below! Shockingly, I became champion of this event and now hold a trophy about as tall as I am, with a winged hound on top.

There is a class called Disposition—the most fun I've ever had. We would joke, we would laugh, we would *dance* among the strangest gullies and floating tables and chairs. Round pieces of cloth filled with hot air carried tiny people in small baskets, and they would cheer for us and play music. Somehow, through all the fun and downright partying, we came out of each lesson more poised and proper.

But even the normal kinds of classes that normal academies taught were extraordinary in Emily. Science was nothing less than scary, and the library of Michelle Tower, where we learned English and History—there has never been a library like it ever. I'm sure of it.

The one class that I did not enjoy was Non-Common Knowledge. We had to face our greatest fears regularly and literally. This was exceedingly difficult for me. I saw my parents die over and over again, and each time, their demise would occur in a new horrific way. Eve Tower was the darkest part of my day. I dreaded it. That was until I received the news that my parents had actually passed away.

Two weeks. Two weeks I was given to mourn. How can anyone be given two weeks for such a thing? Two *years* is hardly enough.

Their death is incredibly mysterious even to this day. The story just isn't quite right. I was told my father killed my mother and then took his own life. This didn't happen. It may have been months since I'd seen them, but my father loved my mother more than anyone in the world. He would never do that. Never.

That day that I received the news of their death was the worst day of my life. But since my greatest fear had been realized, I was now brave enough to do almost anything.

And anything is exactly what I did.

Chapter 20:
Farewell

My eyes blinked open to see my dormitory crowded with academy students, Queen Mothers, and even Queen Delores herself! What in the world? They told me that not only did I die and come back to life, but the Queen Mothers were speaking nonsense about a new Head of Castle...being me!

The room spun a little, and I was nauseous, but as I looked around at all the faces concerned for me and staring at me like I was a ghost, I was overcome with their kindness to come and see me in the middle of the night. I couldn't help smiling. How lovely they all were.

The following week seemed to fly by, and then suddenly, I was bowing to Queen Delores as she crowned me Head Queen of Emily Castle! Everyone cheered and shouted. I thought I'd be sick. But just as I waved to the congregation as the new Head Queen, Queen Delores fell dead on the floor of the Throne Room! I was absolutely distraught. On one of the best days of my life, my parents were not in attendance because they were dead, and now my beloved mentor, whom I had come to trust as a mother, died at the very hour of my crowning.

So it was that the beginning of my reign as Head Queen was a disaster of sorts. But something about pain and suffering makes a new person out of you. A phoenix rises from the ashes.

I took the Head Throne roaring with my wings spread.

All of the things that I had been thinking needed to change, I used my position to change them. First and foremost, I got rid of the cost of tuition and royal robes. Why were we charging people for these things? Everyone who works here at Emily has a grand life, grander than most, with everything they could need and want given to them. The Snickerlings magically provide only the best and rarest ingredients for the most exquisite delicacies to be prepared in Justice Tower. And so, it is! All charging does is exclude those townspeople less fortunate like my parents.

My parents spoke so highly of Pippin, the great White Stag, and it was because of their adoration for him that they felt it necessary to send me to the academy. So next, since no one here seems to notice that the White Stag is behind all of the magic of the castle, not only did I try to do things as maybe a good king like Pippin would, but I also had more of the castle dedicated to him. He still isn't recognized enough, in my opinion.

Because the gown and crown were now free of charge, and so was academy tuition, Batch was always a packed house, and the dormitories were bursting at the seams! I was overjoyed to see everyone and tried so hard to make everyone feel at home, whether they were visiting or permanent residents.

During one Batch, the doctor of Crescent and Fall came to me and humbly proposed the idea of a hospital in the town. Of course, I thought it was a brilliant idea and immediately got the Snickerlings working on it. It is the single best thing that I was able to do as Head Queen.

Ten years. Ten years of ruling the wonderful people of Emily and Crescent and Fall. In those ten years, not only did I host the infamous Em Games—dear reader, these are anything but "games"—but Emily and Crescent and Fall became one. We worked together to accomplish incredible things, and both castle and town had a deep respect for one another.

And that, dear reader, is what I remember as I lie here in the dungeon. I cannot bear the information I have discovered. It has all been revealed to me by none other than the warmouth dragon, Gabriel.

This castle is not the work of Pippin the great White Stag but of Michelle, one of the Chosen, who chose to leave the rest. The dragon spoke so well of him. It was peculiar that he was speaking at all, let alone these strange sayings. Michelle was not a good man but a monster. How can the dragon not see it? And the magic of the castle, it is from the most heinous acts one could ever imagine done to the precious Snickerlings! Those sweet, innocent creatures—my heart is shattered. And if all of that wasn't horrific enough, then Gabriel showed me what has become of my friends

Gus and Martha. Their parents were killed, and Gus and Martha were severely harmed by the hands of men working for Emily!

It is all too much. I cannot bring myself to continue to lead this abomination, and so with this dagger, I take my life. My friends, both in Emily and Crescent and Fall, I leave this letter for you so that you know how much I loved you and that it was a privilege to be your fellow queen.

Farewell, my loves,

Gemma

Chapter 21:
Letter from a
Mighty and Valiant Warrior

"Gus! Gus! You ain't in no condition to be trying to get revenge on anyone!"

Martha didn't understand much. If we let this slide, what those damn hoity toities had done, it would only keep happening to anyone who is a descendant. Gemma didn't know it, but Martha and I knew it now.

"Gus!" she said, "You've lost your head! You'll be killed this time for sure."

"I don't care about that, Martha," I told her. "They murdered our mums and pops in cold blood. I ain't sittin' round letting 'em get away with it."

I stormed out of the pub and down the walk toward the ferry, Martha on my tail. My eye was pounding like a hammer in my skull—or what used to be my eye, anyway. Now, it was just a bloody hole in my head.

Everything was a blur as I stomped through Crescent and Fall to that ole magic boat. I was almost there. Rage was in my veins.

But I was sacked.

A heavy sack fell over me from nowhere, covering my head. Someone's strong arms grasped my body. I couldn't get away, no matter my struggle. Emily had got me easy as that. I'd be seeing my mum and pop pretty soon, after all.

I was dragged for a long while in the leather bag. I was never so glad that it was winter, so hot in that sack. By the darkness, I guessed my kidnappers were taking me into the wood to meet my end. Where was Martha? Did they take her too? I couldn't hear her. I struggled like mad to get out of the sack, but to no avail. Emily had sent their biggest and strongest to do me in.

"Who are ya?" I yelled through the leather.

"Hush, sir," replied a woman's voice. *A lass?* I was ashamed of myself. Either this gal was a big one, or I hadn't lifted enough of those kegs at the pub with my ole pop.

"We aren't going to hurt you," said a man's voice this time. Makes more sense now. Ha! Sure, you won't hurt me.

They dragged me further into the wood before they finally stopped and dumped me out. My eye couldn't believe what it was seeing.

There I sat in the midst of three massive horse-people—two men and a woman—half human, kings and queens to be exact, and half horse!

"Prince Gus!" said one of the men. Both his skin and his horse body were light. "We are the Horsemen. Pippin sent us from Brumbletide. I am Irenaeus, and this is Astrid and James," he said of the queenly horse-woman and the dark and severe kingly horse-man. They both waved a greeting.

"Jumpin' Jiminy, my mind's leaving me," I mumbled.

The Horsemen smiled down at me, looking amused.

"Why have you come?" I asked.

"To help you fight, mighty and valiant warrior," the woman, Astrid, said.

I raised my brow at that. "What ya playin' at? Have ya seen my eye?" I pointed to the bandage Martha plastered on my face.

"Indeed, we did," said the Horsemen, Irenaeus. "And we've heard how hard you fought before losing it."

"Aye, yet I lost it in the end and lost my mum and pop as well. I'm no warrior. Ya got the wrong boy."

"Good warriors never think they are good warriors," said James with a grin.

I grimace. I just can't stand that I lost my mum and pa. "Ya seen Martha? She was on my tail."

Like it was a reply, I heard a mumbling and grumbling, and one of those flying lassies from the castle come flying up with Martha in one arm and her other little hand over her mouth to keep her from screaming.

"Martha!" I shouted

"She is safe!" said Astrid. "Both of you are safe for now."

The winged lass dropped Martha—of course, Martha was flailing all over the place, making It difficult for the lass to set her down gentle.

Martha dusted herself off, face all a fluster. "Whadda ya mean, *for now*? So, you're gonna kill us eventually then?"

The great Horsemen shook their crowned heads, their faces awful solemn.

"No," said the dark horse, James. "We are not going to harm you. We are going to fight by your side in battle."

This account I have written at the request of the Horsemen of Brumbletide who fought by my side during the great Battle of Ipswich (actually, Martha's writing it, I can't write too well.) I'm writing so the truth can be known to the generations to come.

Though it was granted to us that Martha and I would be alive for all of them.

Chapter 22:
The End of All Things

Gemma is gone. I'm stunned! Ten years of planning and preparing—failed attempts to take her life, and then one day, poof! She is gone just like that and not even by my doing. Murdered and taken.

I spread my wings and soar the sky, watching for any movement in the Axiom, the damned abomination that has planted itself in my kingdom. I fly over it daily, watching for any sign of the Six—any sign of the stag.

How am I flying, you ask? Because I am a dragon. My warmouth Gabriel, to be exact. During Gemma's reign, I used the expert counsel of the Dragon on several things. One, I chose a wealthy family from Crescent and Fall to be my figureheads. They will act as Heads of Castle through the ages, doing only as I ask them. The Dragon showed me how he took the life of his warmouth companion to become not only king but *warmouth*. Not only would my doing this unleash power never before seen or wielded, but it would protect me from any uprising that may come to pass. But I work diligently to keep that from happening.

Anguis. Anguis is the name of the family I have chosen as my faithful vessels. They currently have a daughter—a bright pupil in Firebreather House. She will be Head of Castle after her father, who I have been preparing to take the Throne now that Gemma is gone. As of now, my Right Hand is holding things down and has informed the people that their new Head will be crowned soon. Another good thing is that the Anguises are not immortal, so they will be much easier for the people to accept as they only live the lifespan of an average human.

But as I squeeze through the Axiom door, two Snickerlings stand waiting for me in the catacombs. I am outraged. Snickerlings are forbidden to go to the catacombs unless, of course, invited because they have been chosen for sacrifice.

"What are you doing here?" I scowl.

"We apologize, Your Majesty, but we had to come to you at once to make you aware of a peculiar happening."

"What is it?"

"The Lux Sea has turned to blood," breathes the girl.

"Nonsense!" But I am shrouded with dread. I race through the catacombs and up through the dungeon. As I near the secret door, I can already hear worried murmuring in the castle.

When I emerge, everyone is racing and pacing in a panic. Snickerlings gather at the high windows to see the sight. I fly to one of the windows and nose through the wings to get a look. The sea is entirely crimson. Red waves crash into the castle. The ferry bobs along the bloody Lux.

"What is the meaning of this?" And then I almost lose consciousness at the sight that no one seems to be remarking about. Does no one see? Does no one wonder what the ominous line of creatures standing on the wall of Crescent and Fall are doing there? Just standing there looking at the castle. Snickerlings and warmouths—all unfamiliar. Horsepeople! I've seen them only once before. My blood goes cold—even colder than it already is in my current reptile form. These are none other than creatures from Brumbletide! And amidst them all, two humans. I recognize them as the baker's daughter and the bartender's son, who were found to be the harlot's descendants.

Screams of "The end of all things!" screech through the castle. Quickly, I fly to the home of my faithful servant, Cassian Anguis.

Chapter 23:
Letter from One Called
to Be Strong and Courageous

There we stood on that old wall, Martha and me. We were making war with ole Michelle. Snickerlings swarmed the castle, watching us. We were informed that the only ones who would see anything other than Martha and me were the Snickerlings and Michelle. Heck, I didn't see anyone but the five of us! Martha, Irenaeus Imperius, Astrid Oscar, and James Foxenbrand.

There we stood. I had no idea what I was up against. I knew about Gemma, that's all, and that was enough. I knew about Gemma and our mums and dads. That was enough.

By my side was Martha and James, that ole champion. If ya ever find yourself in a fight, you're a lucky dog if ya got James Foxenbrand by your side. Brave as they come, that one.

Suddenly, the dragon came from the castle.

"Michelle's warmouth," said Irenaeus.

Was Michelle sending the beast out to set us ablaze?

"No one move!" shouted Astrid. "Gus, Martha, be strong and courageous! Do not be afraid. You are protected."

We tried to stay strong, but our knees were buckling. The Horsemen knew we were scared something fierce.

"Pippin! If you can hear us, open the eyes of these warriors so they may see!" Irenaeus shouted into the air.

I saw something in my peripheral. White. Martha and I looked to our right and left to see a multitude. Must have been hundreds of Snickerlings hovering over the wall with us! They were children, but they were the most severe children one ever did see.

Martha and I stood taller then. We could take this ole dragon now if it came at us. But the dragon approached us—then flew right over our heads into town. A curious thing.

Chapter 24:
The Mysterious Book

I fly as fast as I can to the house of Anguis. There, I meet Cassian in his courtyard. I lay on my belly, crouching and speaking low. I tell him everything that has happened: how the sea has turned to blood, how everyone is screaming that the end of all things has come. how there is a horde of creatures on the wall staring down the castle.

Anguis is tall and slender with jet-black hair and too-pale skin. He stands, pondering my words with his head bowed and hands clasped behind his back. He seems concerned but not surprised. See, a long while back, while I was still Delores, a book appeared in the castle. It showed up out of nowhere—out of the blue. And not only one but many. At least one was found in every tower; some were found in the Throne Room, some in the dormitories. I had no idea until someone brought me one to inquire about the meaning of a particular passage that seemed to be a prophecy of sorts. It was then I realized what it was. It was from none other than the stag himself. A whole book, a history up until now and what would happen after. I had the Snickerlings confiscate as many as possible, but how much of it had the people had already read?

The lucky nests I've been able to work together for my cause, but the book certainly had no place in Emily. Every single copy must be removed at all costs. But while I kept it from the people, I set my mind to study it and had the Anguises do the same, as they would be carrying on as the face of the Head of Emily. We learned the book backward and forward in order to combat any townspeople who might come speaking it in the congregation.

So, both Cassian and I know the book clearly states that the sea turns to blood before a great and terrible day.

We both sit silently for several minutes, contemplating what to do. Finally, Cassian speaks. "We have to summon the Dragon for assistance."

I sigh. I hate calling on the Dragon and said I wouldn't again. No, I would not be the powerful king I am today without him, but I hate having to call on him for help. It's too close to sharing my kingdom with someone. The Anguises, even on the Throne, are my slaves, but the Dragon is not. He always had an air about him that he thought he was better than me. He was not and is not better than me by any stretch. I have gained more in these few hundred years than he has in millennia. But Cassian is right. If Brumbletide is coming to fight Emily, I will need all the power of my kingdom and any I can get from anywhere else as well.

And so, we called the Dragon. I flew Anguis on my back to the castle, high in the air so as not to stir up the creatures on the wall that were *still* there. We flew to the dungeon and into the catacombs. There, we summoned the Dragon.

He arrives quietly in a puff of smoke. He is quiet and solemn, a very different disposition for him. What is wrong?

"Dragon," I say, "we need your assistance in fighting this army that has risen against us."

"All is lost," he says.

Anguis and I stare. I can tell dread has settled on Anguis, too, at the Dragon's words. A chill runs through me all the way to the tip of my tail, although I'm not sure why.

"All is lost, Sire?" asks Anguis.

"Maybe not for you. Not for now. But for me, the sand has run out. I will help you if I can but know this will be the final time."

What is he saying? "Nonsense, Dragon, you are losing heart. We can win if we team together."

"That is what he wants you to think. The sad thing is we really believe we can win until the time arrives when all comes clean."

"Nonsense, Dragon," I say.

In the Dungeon, Anguis and I assemble our Snickerling army, and about a thousand of the Dragon's Sinckerlings appear as well. Snickerlings are packed in the dungeon and the catacombs, all hovering, ready to fight at our word. Our army is vast and powerful—we dwarf the creatures on the wall many times over.

Chapter 25:
Letter from One
of the Boggletrice Company

There we were, the Brumbletide army and Martha and I still standing there staring at that ole castle. We even saw that ole dragon fly right over us again, but the Horsemen told us to hold yet still. We did nothing but stand there on that wall staring at that Emily over the bloody Lux. Strangest thing we'd ever seen or done.

And then we went home.

After all that standing and staring, we went home to the pub that was now in my care because my mum and pa were gone. But the Horsemen came with us. They set a fire burning in the fireplace and then had us walk right through just like we were at Emily. But this fire wasn't a strange fire—it burned a righteous flame. We walked through it into what became our meeting place. The Horseman called us the Boggletrice Company. I had no clue what it meant and still don't to this day. But I had no clue what was in store for the Boggletrice Company either. Couldn't have imagined it in my wildest dreams. Never in my wildest.

Three days we stood on that wall. Three days just standing there staring it down. But on the fourth...

Chapter 26:
The Tempest

Three days. Three days we kept our Snickerling army hidden away in the dungeon and catacombs until battle broke out and they were needed.

Three days the Brumbletide creatures just stood there watching us but doing nothing. I had the castle on lockdown. No one could come or go. However, classes resumed as usual and no one mentioned anything except that a young man and woman were standing on the wall. For some reason, they can't see the creatures. Why?

But now, on the fourth day, Anguis and I go to the balcony. I sense a dreadful feeling that has shrouded us both. There they are as they have been. Waiting. Watching.

At this point, my nerves have settled a good deal since they haven't done anything but stand and watch. It is becoming more apparent that they do not know what they will do. They do not know how or if they will attack. Still, I am uneasy. We watch the creatures for a bit more before going back into the castle. But just as we do, a sound comes from the wall.

We rush to the edge of the balcony in a panic but calm down once we look. Of the mass of creatures, the sound comes from the two *humans*. They are jumping up and down and screaming their heads off. What in the name? Anguis and I watch in sheer surprise before exchanging a glance and bursting into laughter.

But our laughter halts as a much louder, shrill, piercing sound joins the two screaming idiots. We look to see that the Snickerlings have stretched out their arms to their sides, and their mouths are round with sound. I feel a strange tugging as if a swift wind has caught hold of me. I draw my wings in as close to my body as they will go as not to be swept away. But then the Horsemen sing. *Sing!* And Anguis and I watch, awestruck in horror. When the song of the Horsemen joins the others, a visible, swirling wind erupts from their mouths, and Anguis and I are sucked off of the balcony and are now bumbling through the air like autumn leaves. And again, to our great terror, out of the castle windows blows our Snickerling army all the way from the depths of the dungeon and even the catacombs! They pour out of the windows and tumble like tumbleweeds around the castle. When every single one is sucked outside, the creatures then abruptly stop their singing and rush our army for battle. The Snickerlings take flight. The Horsemen ride right on top of the water as if dry ground, and the two idiot humans stand on the wall—as if they could do anything at all!

The Brumbletide Snickerlings are slaying both the Emily Snickerlings and the Dragon's! Ours drop like flies. New ones appear in their place but, startled by the immediate danger, fly off to safety. *No! I need those!*

In dragon form, I speak to the Snickerlings in an ancient language only known by them and myself these days. "Stand down!" I yell in desperation. "Find safety however you can!" Then, seeing that they are following my orders, I dive into the Lux with Anguis on my back and stay just deep enough in the water for Anguis to come up for air now and then.

From under the castle, I watch my Snickerlings dive into the sea and escape back into the castle windows until all that is left are the Brumbletide creatures and the two humans again. The humans have done nothing this whole time. The Horsemen and Snickerlings line the wall again. Their mouths drop.

Oh no.

The shrill song blasts a whirlwind—a monstrous, grey tempest toward my castle. It covers Emily completely, seeping into every window, doorway, nook, and crevice. In a second, the conical roof of Michelle Tower opens, and the Dragon is sucked out the top. The tempest holds the Dragon helpless in midair.

Watching the Dragon who mentored me so well for centuries now hanging defenseless, his words ring in my mind again, "All is lost."

And then, the wind leaves the mouths of the creatures and begins to take shape all on its own. I can't quite make out the figure, but it seems to be a creature of sorts—something *alive*.

The Dragon's eyes roll wide in his head. He is terrified. How strange a sight! Streams of wind elongate and become thick, more palpable, more visible. Legs. Those are legs—four legs. A head.

I lose my breath. *Antlers*. Massive, spiking, razor-sharp *antlers*.

The stag.

The stag, fifty times his natural size, walks through the tempest as if it were a stroll in the wood on a spring day. He lowers his head. My eyes grow wide, and I scream, my shout muffled under water.

The great antlers stab through the helpless Dragon and come out the other end, dripping with blood. The stag pulls back his head, and the Dragon falls dead into the sea.

Multitudes. Thousands upon thousands of Snickerlings rise from the bloody sea and fly off in various directions. When the last of them has gone, the sea returns to its natural blueish green.

The stag walks to the creatures, who stroke him affectionately and kiss him on the nose just before he vanishes.

Anguis and I stay where we are until the creatures and men are gone. My worst fear has been realized, and Emily still stands.

Universe, your face shines upon me.

Chapter 27:
Letter from One Who Saw the Battle of Ipswich

Pippin, that great King, had slayed the Dragon, that deceiver from ancient times. We asked Pippin to stay, to come back with us to the Boggletrice Company hideout, but he had to go.

"Your Majesty," I found the nerve to say, "we sure are grateful for what you've done. But Emily still stands, and Michelle is still alive."

"Indeed, Prince Gus of Fairfang. The root has been destroyed. Emily's harvest is appointed." He looked to everyone. "This land will no longer be called Crescent and Fall, but Little Ipswich."

The Boggletrice Company exchanged smiles at that as Pippin disappeared before our very eyes. But when he did, something dropped in the place where he had been standing. Irenaeus picked it up and held it for all of us to examine. It was a long rod of gold with many stones at the end; the biggest in the center was a shining white pearl. We all marveled at the Scepter, though it gave every one of us a funny feeling.

"My word," said Astrid.

"Leviathan," said James. "There are legends of it, but it was never told that it holds the stones of the Seven and Pippin himself!"

Irenaeus looked at the Scepter, which shone brightly now. "Would you look at that? What a gift!" But in his eyes was greed, which now I know all too well.

But those mighty Horsemen denied the pull of the Scepter and left Leviathan in my care. Because of it, Martha and I do not age like everyone else as long as we come in contact with it once a day. Our progression toward death is much slower than natural. It protects us, too, from anyone up to no good—it renders them blind to us. That is how Martha and I have remained alive for over two hundred years.

And as for Crescent and Fall, it has been known as Little Ipswich ever since that fateful day.

Chapter 28:
Glory Days

Even now, in my disembodied state, six hundred years later, I love reliving the days of my glory. The days I physically sat on the Head Throne of Emily, the greatest kingdom there ever was and ever will be. But to have raised up figureheads to hold down my place as I worked tirelessly to create the miracle that is Emily Castle, to have extracted so much blood with my bare hands in order to unleash more magic than has ever before been wielded, and to infiltrate and infuse the townspeople without them suspecting a thing—it is the work of an extraordinary genius. The work I was called to do from the beginning of time.

Yet, the Dragon is gone, and I could easily suffer the same fate. That fateful day that the stag slew the Dragon—it was a gift that I saw it, a blessing from the Universe. I've replayed it daily in my mind, each time just as vivid as when my eyes first beheld it.

Would the stag come for *me*?

I couldn't leave it to chance. I pondered and pondered the possibility. I obsessed to the point that I incessantly schemed ways to combat him if he arrived one day, coming for me as he did the Dragon.

Several Anguises have sat on the Head Throne now. They have served me faithfully. Yet, I grew too comfortable with their loyalty, and they have gone awry in recent years with Lenore even bringing up the stag in her Batch addresses! It has been said they are only slaying one Snickerling a year—nowhere near enough. But this proved necessary as while the Anguises were doing my bidding, I was able to travel the world, searching high and low for the remedy to the disease that is the stag.

I found it in a man named Klauschwitz.

It turned out that the Universe played a hand in connecting Anguis and me so long ago. It knew that it was by a relation of this family that my life would be saved even if my body was no more.

Charleston Anguis brought a report one day of his cousin who resided in China and knew a woman who kept an extraordinary zoo of animals—all with wings.

Warmouths.

Anguis said if we could get those warmouths to a scientist headmaster of an almost ancient school in Germany, he could infuse his extraordinary war-trained students with the blood of the warmouths to make a superior race. Not only could we build an army more powerful than any other, but he also had worked for years studying the Shame Plant, a flower that binds the heart to its deepest desires. For centuries, I had expertly crafted Emily in such a way similar that not only did the majority of Crescent and Fall desire Emily and its ways more than anything else, but now I myself had become one with the castle as Emily is my greatest desire.

I went with a team of faithful Snickerlings, and we found the woman in China. Her zoo was exactly as Anguis had said. She had hundreds of warmouths that she trained and exploited for financial gain. It was easy to steal them. In fact, they seemed relieved to see their fellow creatures, the Snickerlings, and came willingly. We didn't have to bind them; they flew freely with us to Germany, where Klauschwitz was eagerly waiting. In the centuries since the debacle of Gemma, the ancient Infernum Academy has raised a breed of extraordinary royal students. While I have never counted the townspeople as true royalty, though they don their ridiculous costumes at Batch and in the academy, this race is true royalty in my eyes, and they shall fight for their kingdom. As for the Emily "royals," Klauschwitz has now perfected the extraction of the magic of the Shame Plant. It is infused into the feasts of Emily, solidifying the subject's loyalty and making them nothing more than my vessels. The beauty of this is that once the Shame is in the body, it is then passed down to the descendants. By Lenore's reign, we no longer needed much of the Shame Plant but used it anyway for good measure.

Everything was in order. If the stag ever did come to slay me, I would live on not only in Emily Castle but in the very hearts of those who love it.

And so, here I dwell, more powerful and able than ever because while before I was restrained to only one body, now I have thousands.

One thing I did not consider is that my power would be significantly diminished in the mortals because even though they consume trace amounts of Snickerling blood in their feasts, they do not consume anywhere near the amount that I did in the catacombs.

So now that the event has happened—the stag did, in fact, come. I must now get the academy students and the townspeople to become as I once was—bodies of flesh and blood full of my power.

My servants, my vessels, my army.

The Einsreich will ensure this comes to pass.

Chapter 29:
Obsidian

"Speechless," is all I can say in response to the story we've just heard.

We are in the Boggletrice Company headquarters, sipping cocoa and munching on winter wedding cakes while waiting for Atticus and Calysta to recover from the prolonged starvation and thirst they experienced in the dungeon. I like to save winter wedding cakes for special occasions since they were a special treat between Grandma and me. I can't think of a more special occasion than with the Six, a pile of sleeping warmouths, and the Boggletrice Company minus King McShanihan, who has yet to turn up.

The ancestors! I still can't believe I am sitting here with them! Jericho, Gus, Martha, Queen Lenore, Wes, Jack, Atticus, Calysta, and I were all captured by Thorn and put in the dungeon. At the same time, Thorn's father, Tritch Anguis, and King Klauschwitz took over Emily with their evil, red-eyed, zombie academy royals, the Einsreich. Thankfully, Justice's warmouth sparrow, Theary, retrieved all of the ancestor's stolen stones and took them to Brumbletide so the Six could come out of the Axiom and rescue us. And rescue us they did—with a horde of warmouths of various kinds, big and small, massive and tiny. The Einsreich are so powerful because they are infused with the magical blood of warmouths—but because of this, warmouths can defeat them. We escaped the castle and came here to the Boggletrice Company headquarters, a magical hideaway you can only get to through the fire in the fireplace in Gus's pub, The Lazy Jug.

The Six and the Horsemen have just finished telling Wes, Jack, Lenore, and me the long story of Michelle's reign through the centuries. My mind whirls with these new terrible revelations, and especially with the death of Gemma! How in the world am I supposed to do this if *she* couldn't do it? She was the closest thing to perfection there was!

"I can't believe Gemma took her own life," I say solemnly. "Are you sure? It wouldn't be out of the realm of possibility that Emily killed her and made it look like she took her life."

"Then why would the legends say she was murdered?" asks Jack. "Wouldn't Emily want to deflect blame from themselves?"

Jack being here is another thing that I can't believe. I'm glad, but the butterflies in my belly are annoying.

"Not this time. Gemma was so beloved, they knew the people would question more if she had taken her own life because whatever it was that made her do it would have had to be something utterly horrific," says King Justice of his descendant.

"I can vouch that is a correct assessment," says Lenore.

"Mortimer took her body but left a note," adds Queen Eve. Gemma is a descendant of both Eve and Justice.

"King McShanihan?" Jack and I say together.

"He was alive then?" I ask.

"Whatever happened to him? He disappeared when the Einsreich came," says Wes.

The ancestors and Horsemen smile at us, amused at all of our questions.

"So many questions! One at a time, friends," grins Queen Sara Lisa.

"Aquila told Mortimer what happened. He would ask about Gemma from time to time. He went from here," Sara Lisa indicates the round, red door in the cottage-like room that leads into a long corridor of strange, decorated doors leading to many different places, "snuck into the dungeon and took her."

"Where?" asks Jack.

"We don't know," replies King George, who has had a much sunnier disposition since rescuing us from the dungeon. He and Henry the Horsemen get along very well.

"But is he immortal?" I ask.

Flori beams. "Aye, no beginning and no end—full of ancient wisdom, he is."

"That's not true. King McShanihan told Atticus and me his Mum and Dad took him to the Em games when he was a boy."

"Indeed. Even immortals desire a family, whether they are blood-related or not. And Mortimer is the most powerful royal Pippin has ever chosen, so he can change his appearance and even his age at will," Justice tells us. "But though he will not die naturally, he can be killed. That is why he will disappear from time to time. It is better for him to hide sometimes so that he will keep living on to help those who need him."

It makes a little sense, but something about it nags at me. It seems strange to just run away.

"Is he hiding now?" I ask.

My very many times over great grandmother, Eve, rubs my back. "He could be, but we don't think so because he took the Scepter, Darling. He would never do that knowing that the Scepter keeps Gus and Martha from aging like everyone else."

Gus grunts. "Well, we ain't kicked the bucket yet. I ain't givin' up fightin' until there ain't any air left in these lungs."

"Come on, Gus. The Scepter wasn't even working the way it had been before. That Emily man was able to see you when he was killing Maggie's father."

Gus lowers his head as a pit sinks in my stomach, and a lump forms in my throat. Dad. I can't believe he hasn't crossed my mind that much with all that's been going on in and out of the castle. I do miss him so much. Eve squeezes my hand.

"I will not lie to you; the ache never goes away completely. But not everyone gets to feel love so deeply that when the loved one is gone, the hurt never leaves." Eve envelopes me in her arms. My eyes begin to gush, and I quietly cry into her gown.

"Oh, dearie, how careless of me," says Martha sadly. "Forgive me, Maggie."

I sit up and wipe my eyes. "It's alright, Martha, really. I was just feeling guilty because I haven't thought about him much lately."

"The human mind is a funny thing—a fascinating thing," says Queen Soleil, who is known for the science tower of Emily Academy. "Don't be down on yourself, Princess. You've been a little busy lately." She smiles warmly. It's good to hear her voice. She hasn't said much at all, and that is probably because hearing the terrible tale of how her twin brother betrayed Pippin and built the evilest abomination there ever was wasn't the most joyous of pastimes. At second glance, I see that her eyes have tears too. For Soleil to look sad is a stark contrast from her usual cheery disposition. "I do understand, Princess. Imagine being *glad* your loved one is gone. I did love him once."

The only person I can compare this to is Mum. I have wished she was dead before, but I wonder how I would feel if it really happened. Magnus sleepily flies up and gives my cheek a soft nuzzle, bringing a smile to my tear-stained face.

"Right," says George. "Let's trade one tragic topic for another, shall we? Our little friends will be up and well again soon, so we need to plan our attack so that we can get going as soon as possible. Those demon children aren't going to wait around to start wreaking havoc."

"Right," I say, "and who knows what Thorn's dad has already done. He is dangerous enough even without the Einsreich."

While I was recovering from a nasty head injury, my dormmate, Thorn, took over Head of Castle (I was previously Head of Emily Castle. I know, ridiculous.) Thorn's dad, Tritch Anguis, brought in a bunch of demon kids called the Einsreich that look like Emily royals but are huge and super strong due to having been infused with warmouth blood at their home academy, Infernum. Because of the warmouth blood, warmouths are pretty much the only thing that can work against them, but there are a lot more of the Einsreich than there are of warmouths, and as far as I can see, we humans aren't worth much of a fight. The stones keep the ancestors alive and do hold powers that I have seen used at times, but I don't know how to work them, and I haven't seen the crown stones do *that* much anyway. Not to mention, the stones were stolen so easily at the Changing of the Crowns ceremony. I shudder remembering the Six's withering bodies aging decades in seconds. "We have to keep your stones safe this time. Can we glue them into your crowns?"

The Six smile knowingly. "Thought you'd never ask," says Justice smartly. "Pippin was waiting with us when Theary brought the first few stones. He told us to go to The Resplendent to the shoe shop. The Snickerlings there would know what to do."

"I was the first," beams Sara Lisa. "Behold!" She raises her perfect bare foot in the air so that all of us can see the bottom. There, implanted into her sole, is her ruby!

"My word," breathes Jack, examining her heel. "Is it painful?"

"Not a bit," Sara Lisa replies giddily. "And now, we can come and go as we please!"

"Wonderful!" I exclaim. This is the best news I've heard in my life. "But you all have stones in your crowns too."

"They are just regular stones so no one questions," says Eve. "The power still streams between the stone and the crown." She draws an imaginary line with her finger from her foot to her head.

"Fascinating," Wes breathes. Lenore's arms are tightly crossed. She looks somewhat jealous to me, but that may be my imagination.

"We come bearing gifts," says Flori brightly. From her coat's many pockets, she removes several opaque, blood-red stones. Jack and I exchange curious looks, even though I have a feeling I know what these are for. And if I'm right, this is unbelievable.

Flori sets several stones on the table before us. "Obsidian from Pippin. One for you, Maggie." She presses one of the stones into the groove in my crown that once held Eve's lapis lazuli. A pulse of warm power rushes through me, and I sit up tall. "One for you, Jack." Flori does the same for Jack's simple gold crown and then Wes's. Both of their expressions brighten as the power pulses through them too.

"We have one for everyone. Gus, Martha, Lenore, and two for Princess Calysta and Prince Atticus when they wake."

"What's everyone up to?" says a groggy voice from the bed.

"Calysta! You're awake!" I run to her and gently hug my dear friend whom I almost lost for good a second time. She was turned to stone when she bravely defeated Medusa in the Em Games, and then she and Atticus nearly starved to death in the dungeon. Her black hair pokes every which way out of her tiara. She isn't out of place. All of us are in tattered gowns that have seen much better days.

Eve brings Calysta's obsidian and kisses her forehead. "You're just in time, Princess." She holds the obsidian for Calysta to see and then replaces the tiara's front diamond with it. A glow returns immediately to Calysta's face.

"Thank you, Your Majesty," she tells Eve. "I feel brand new!"

"Wonderful," laughs Eve.

Calysta looks across the bed at Atticus, who is still sleeping soundly. "Will he be alright?"

"Yes," says Justice. "Jericho has been feeding you both broth while you slept, and we could tell you were improving. He just needs his rest."

"In the meantime, Gus, Martha, retrieve your crowns, please," orders Eve with a grin.

Gus and Martha wore their royal garments like the rest of us when we were taken to the dungeon, but both of them had removed their crowns the second we got to the headquarters. They are not used to dressing like this like the rest of us are, and Gus especially hates it. I can tell Gus wants to resist, but they both do as Eve asks and in a moment, they too have obsidian stones in their crowns.

"Thank you kindly, your majesties," says Martha.

"Yes, thank you, my queens and kings," says Gus with a bow.

"The pleasure is ours, grandson—especially Pippin's," reminds Sara Lisa.

We all huddle around Calysta at the table, trying our best to catch her up on the story quickly. Atticus grunts and turns but doesn't wake. The Horsemen cuddle up in a pile on the floor for a nap with Felixus, Magnus, and some of the other warmouths that came to our rescue in the dungeon.

Chapter 30:
Everly Drive

An hour later, Atticus wakes up, and he, too, is overjoyed to receive the obsidian in his crown. His pale face immediately becomes rosy. He joins us at the table and slowly eats the hearty meal of pumpkin dumplings, courtesy of Jericho. I can tell he wants to devour everything at once, but he doesn't because it will all come up again.

The rest of us do not eat or drink; our minds gearing up for whatever is ahead.

"You all now have eternity stones," says George. "But it is crucial to remember that you can still die. You will never die of natural causes as long as you keep in contact with the stone, but it is quite possible for you to die of unnatural causes. Remember this in battle and do everything you can to stay alive."

Several of us gulp through the nervous tension that has settled in at George's warning.

"Are we going to fight tonight?" Atticus asks George. He has put his fork down and raised out of his seat.

"I like your vigor, young man, but some tasks must be done before fighting."

"Right," says Justice. "We must find King McShanihan."

"Indeed," says Sara Lisa. "But we need to stop by home. Look at their gowns. One wrong move, and they'll come clean off!" She exposes a torn hole in the torso of Jack's gown, which makes him blush.

"What are you playing at, Sara?" pipes George. "We can't go back to the castle! There are more Einsreich in that place than bees in a hive. Absolutely not!"

"He's right, Your Majesty," says Gus. "We won't be goin' back to the Axiom unless Pippin happens to bring it out by chance. I'm sure Martha and I can come up with something for them to wear."

The other kids and I look at one another, knowing what we all are thinking. Both Atticus and Jack are taller and thinner than Gus, and Calysta and I are bigger and taller than Martha.

"Uh, how about we just go to someone's house and get some clothes?" says Atticus. "We're safe as long as we aren't in the castle."

"Don't be so sure of that," says Flori. "You're *safer* than in Emily, but safe? No. Watchers are everywhere."

"It isn't a bad idea for them to get some clothes from their homes," says Sara Lisa.

I wince at her words. I never want to return to the house on Everly that I certainly do not consider a home, clothes or no clothes.

"Maggie and I aren't too far from here. We can get things from our houses. Calysta can wear something of Maggie's and—" Atticus eyes Jack's broad shoulders and brawny build. "I'm sure my dad has something for you."

Eve notices my worried expression. "It will be alright, darling. I will come too."

Her warmth melts much of my worry.

Eve looks around at the other ancestors at the table. "I am going to chaperone my granddaughter and her friends. We'll bring back things for Lenore and Wesley."

Gus warns her to be extremely cautious and to try not to stand out. He jumps up and grabs some bulky coats from the coat rack. "Wear these. The town has seen Emily royals a bunch of times before. The coats will cover most of the rips and stains."

"He's right, dearies," says Martha, pulling more coats from the wardrobe.

The next thing we know, Calysta, Jack, Atticus, Eve, and I are all standing by the Boggletrice Company fireplace dressed in Gus's bulky pea coats and Martha's fitted furs.

"Splendid!" Martha exclaims.

The fire cracks and grows in the fireplace, and Ignatius's distinguished voice comes from it. "Hello, Company! Looks like you are on your way out. Don't let me hold you up. Come on through, don't be shy."

As we enter the fire, we hear a gasp from the flames and stop.

"What? What is it, Ignatius?"

"Oh-oh, it's nothing. Be on your way! Hi-hello, all. He-hello again, Queen Sara Lisa." There is sadness in his voice.

"Greetings again, Ignatius," replies Sara Lisa joyfully, obviously oblivious that Ignatius is Boris, her husband who betrayed her and stole her child away from her so many years ago.

"Looks like we might miss a juicy conversation," I say to Eve on the other side. The pub is dark and empty. It's been closed for weeks.

"Whatever do you mean?" she replies, and I remember that none of the ancestors know who Boris was before.

"I'll tell you on the way. It's a doozy."

She raises a brow as we exit the pub and start down the sidewalk toward the bridge. The others lead the way, and Eve and I hang behind. "When I was in the castle's hospital, the Queen's Doctor told me that Ignatius is Boris, Sara Lisa's husband!" I whisper to her.

Eve's dainty mouth drops. "Boris!" she whispers. "You're sure?"

"He even confirmed it himself, and Gus came and called him 'granddad'! It was all so strange but true. He feels terrible and hates everything he did. Pippin has him in the castle as a spy."

"That's brilliant! Pippin knows how to turn around even the worst of situations. But I can't imagine Sara Lisa taking the news lightly."

"I can't either."

"We shall see, won't we?"

"We shall," I reply.

We lock arms and hurry behind the others to the bridge.

It is late afternoon on a Thursday, so Downtown Ipswich is pretty empty. We pass a few townspeople that give us only a sideways glance. When we pass the bakery, it has a whole new air now. The windows are dark, and a sign reading "closed" is hanging on the door. Before, it was just a bakery with the best pipers around. Now, it is a bakery that was invisible to castle officials by the magic of the Scepter with an immortal owner made of sugar and spice.

"I rarely come here. It's been ages," Atticus says of Downtown Ipswich. "I've lived in the castle for years now. You start to forget what real life is like. How ordinary people live."

"Ordinary is often the most extraordinary," offers Eve.

We cross the bridge over the Lux, where I heard words from Pippin's Puzzle speaking to me from the water the night I ran away. That seems so long ago, but we haven't even gotten through the Winter Semester—and it looks like there is a good chance we might not.

Way too soon, we arrive in the Ipswich Hills neighborhood and round the corner to Everly Drive. Atticus and Jack go on to the Peabody residence, and Eve and Calysta follow me up the driveway to Mum's dark, empty home filled with so many bitter memories.

Eve brightens. "How quaint," she says positively.

I try the door—locked.

"I'm going to have to go through the back window. It's okay. I did it all the time after school when Mum would lock us out."

"Did she work?" asked Calysta.

"No, she was home."

The three of us go behind the house, and Calysta and Eve watch as I remove the screen and lift the kitchen window. I climb in, step into the sink, and jump onto the floor.

"Go to the side door, and I'll let you in," I tell them.

"Alright, darling."

On the way to the side door, I hear a murmuring from the direction of the living room. The hair rises on my neck. What in the world could it be? The van isn't in the drive. Mum's in jail, and if it were Dad, I think I would faint and die too. Before letting Eve and Calysta in, I slowly push the swinging door to the living room. The noise comes from the television that is tuned to American reruns. My mother is passed out on the floor with a cigarette burning in an ashtray on the coffee table and snack wrappers strewn about. She has gained probably a hundred pounds.

I gaze in shock until I remember Eve and Calysta and run back through the swinging door, quickly letting them in.

"What's wrong, Maggie? You look like you've seen a ghost!" says Calysta.

"Worse," I say, pushing the swinging door open and revealing the pile on the floor that is my mother.

Chapter 31: Margaret

"This is your mum you told us about?" asks Calysta, unable to pull her gaze away from the slobbering lump on the floor.

Eve gently pushes us toward the stairs. "My word. Come girls, this is not for young eyes."

"She wasn't *quite* like that when I saw her last. She was smaller and more...kept."

The three of us start up the stairs, but a moaning follows halfway up. We stop and turn to see Mum stirring and gurgling.

"Is she alright? Should we call an ambulance?" asks Calysta in alarm.

Mum's eyes blink open. She slowly lifts her head and grunts as she finally sits up after a few tries. *"AAAAAAAAAAHHHHHHH!"*

Calysta, Eve, and I scream too.

"Don't move! I'm calling the police!" Mum shouts. She rolls over to the phone by the recliner. Several snack wrappers crunch underneath her on the way.

"Mum, don't! It's me!" I shout.

"Exactly why I'm calling the authorities. Eye for an eye, you little witch!"

At once, a bolt of blue light bursts from the staircase, knocking the phone out of Mum's hands. Mum screams and ducks, throwing her arms over her head. "What the hell was that?"

"You will not speak in that way to your daughter again," says Eve, who has descended into the living room and stands between my mother and Calysta and me.

"You, ma'am, are a selfish and ungrateful swine of a woman, and I will not allow you to treat Maggie as you have been." Eve's eyes are dead set on the cowering lump by the recliner.

At this, Mum lowers her arms a bit and smirks. "Well, I see Maggie's already fooled you too, whoever you are—a witch, I suspect. Look at me. That girl has ruined my life! We were a perfect family before she just *had* to get her way. She *begged* me to take her to Emily, and not only did I not get so much as a 'thank you,' but she crashed our household into the ground, and everyone but Maggie burned up in flames. My husba—"

Blue light blasts at Mum's feet, burning a hole in the carpet. Mum squeals and jumps behind the recliner.

"I understand what it means to be a terrible mother. But when it is in your power to do so, it is your duty to try to change— to try to be a good one."

Mum's voice comes from the recliner. "Ha! She's got you fooled, lady. She's not an expert in much, but she's a master of manipulation. Better watch your back, or you'll end up like the rest of us."

Eve holds her gaze on the recliner. "You see no wrong-doing of your own?"

"Not to toot my own horn, but I'm the glue that held this family together—the rock foundation. This family wouldn't have made it as far as we did without me. But when something so determined to destroy it all refuses to give up until it's all gone—not even the savior can keep it from going to hell."

Eve glances back at me with a look as if she happened upon a rabid bunny and feels bad that it has to be put down. Her shoulders slump, realizing there is no way to get through to this woman. "Then, by your words, you shall be judged. I forbid you ever to come looking for Maggie again. If you do, you will pay dearly."

"Pfft, don't worry your fancy head about me looking for her. Never in million." But then somehow, Mum gets a wind of bravery. "But who's gonna keep me from coming for her if I ever did get the whim, huh?"

Eve stands tall and speaks clearly and authoritatively. "Queen Eve the Wise. Royalty in the Order of Pippin the Great, and great ancestor of the beloved Princess Maggie Prewitt of Ironsnout."

There is silence for several seconds before the recliner speaks. "Maggie, where did you find this witch buffoon of insanity? Get whatever you came for and get out."

Eve nods to me. "Go on, girls. I'll watch her."

Calysta and I scurry to my room. I dig through my wardrobe, and in a few minutes, Calysta and I are wearing tattered jeans that are a little oversized and T-shirts that advertise companies we've never heard of.

"Sorry, she only buys used things for Wes and me."

Calysta shrugs. "Well, at least we don't have to worry about getting them dirty."

We stand side by side in front of my wardrobe mirror. Two preteen girls wearing ratty charity shop garb and magnificent royal crowns. We laugh and then grab something for Wes to wear from his room.

"We need something for Lenore," says Calysta. "Do you have anything?"

I think for a moment until I remember something of Mum's that will suit Lenore perfectly.

I go into Mum's room. It's a mess. I've never seen it like this. The bed is unmade, clothes strewn all over the floor, cigarettes are piled in ashtrays on the end tables. But hanging in her closet is the purple garment bag from Emily that holds the gown and crown she bought for herself when she took Wes and me to Batch for the first and only time. I grab the garment bag, and Calysta and I fly down the stairs to Eve, who still guards the recliner. She waits for us to open the swinging door to the kitchen before telling Mum. "Remember my warning, and quit smoking. It's disgusting." With that, she hurries after us out the door.

"Whew! Glad that's done," says Calysta, giving me a high five.

My heart leaps at Eve's protection and Calysta's friendship. The three of us run down the drive to meet the boys in the street.

Mrs. Peabody didn't question the boys much, completely believing Atticus's story that he and Jack needed commonwealth clothing for a project in Hospitality. Still, she was horrified at the state of his gown, which left Atticus having to lie even more, saying that even that was part of the project. Atticus is now dressed in jeans and a yellow Champion sweatshirt. Jack is dressed the same way except for a good portion of his forearms and ankles showing out of the sleeves and pant legs. Calysta and I can't help but giggle.

"Hey!" says Jack, blushing. "It's better than a torn-up gown."

"It will work just fine," Eve encourages. "Now, hurry along, everyone. We must get back to the Company."

Chapter 32:
Memories

The five of us walk back to the Boggletrice Company in solemn silence. I'm willing to bet each of us is trying in our heads to come up with a way to solve our problem but coming up with nothing.

When we reach the pub, there is now a nervous tension amongst us. Felixus and Magnus greet us happily on the other side of the fireplace with nuzzles and hoots. The Horsemen and most of the warmouths are awake. Anastasia and Martha are cooking in the kitchen. Henry and Cornelius sip coffee while warmouths gently wrestle and play around them. Fergus lopes at full speed toward Atticus with a stream of slobber trailing behind his head and pins him to the ground, licking his face profusely. "Ah! Good boy! Blimey, that's a lot of drool," Atticus laughs, scratching Fergus's ears.

Jack holds his finger out, and Theary perches on it, tweeting happily. Zelda, Soleil's lumpy white dragon, rubs against Calysta's leg, wanting pets, which Calysta happily obliges. Sara

Lisa's panther, Hildi, is too busy trying to get Flori's beaver Teddy's heavy tail off her back as he still sleeps peacefully beside her, unaware of any commotion.

The others have made a feast worthy of Emily—or Brumbletide, I should say. There are hot rolls are dripping with butter, a mound of mashed potatoes, mushy peas, and a sizzling pork loin in the center, to which Magnus wildly squeaks his protest.

"Who's hungry?" asks Anastasia, her human torso and some of her front horse legs covered by an apron.

All of us kids reply, "Me!" and rush to the table. The ancestors, Horsemen, children, Gus, Martha, Lenore, and Jericho enjoy a wonderful dinner together, with warmouths flying overhead and cuddled up to feet below, occasionally getting handed a bite under the table.

When everyone is either having ice cream, coffee, or Bubblegin, Justice brings up what will happen next. "This has been a lovely time, but we must discuss important matters."

Everyone sulks except George, Henry, and Atticus—the Champions.

"We have two missions to execute. One group needs to find McShanihan, and the other needs to gather intel from Emily," says George.

"Intel?" asks Justice.

"It's a modern term for information," George explains. "Henry told me." He slaps Henry on his horse back. Henry's hooves clop in response.

"Alright, yes. We've been discussing it while you all were away, and we think it's best if two ancestors go with the children to look for McShanihan and the other four of us will go to the castle to see what's going on."

"What? No! You'll be killed!" I exclaim. I want to rid Emily of Michelle's evil just as much as the others, but I do not want to lose the ancestors again.

"Don't worry, Princess," says Justice calmly. "Batch is coming up. We'll blend in with all the other royals."

I can see how it would be difficult to spot them amid hundreds of royally dressed townspeople, but I'm still worried.

"Where are we supposed to look for King McShanihan?" asks Calysta.

"We don't know, Princess," says Soleil. "He could be anywhere around the world."

"We don't have time to look all the way around the world!" I exclaim impatiently, immediately feeling terrible that I said this to Soleil, who is always pleasant. "Sorry, Soleil. I'm just...you know. This is a lot!"

Soleil smiles sympathetically. "I understand, Princess Maggie. It is."

Eve places her hand on mine. "The good news is when a true Brumbletisian is lost, Brumbletide ensures they are found. We've just got to start looking."

I squeeze Eve's hand, a little encouraged but not much.

"Alright, who will go with the children to find Mortimer? Who will go to Batch?" asks Flori, Teddy now curled up in her lap. She strokes his flat, leathery tail.

"We are going with the children too," says Henry, indicating Anastasia and Cornelius. "You'll be going by night, so we won't be seen. And when we do find McShanihan, he can change us back. But we will be a great help to the group on the way."

"Alright, Henry, but you have to make sure no one sees you," says Justice. "How about Eve and Sara Lisa go with the children, and Flori, George, Soleil, and I will go to the castle?"

Everyone agrees that is a reasonable plan.

"Gus and Martha, you two stay here with Lenore. She will stick out too much wherever she goes. The three of you watch over the headquarters. And open up your shops so that the townspeople don't begin to suspect something."

Gus bows his head to Justice. "Will do, King."

"Don't forget to use your stones if trouble comes," George reminds them.

Wes, Calysta, Atticus, Jack, and I all exchange an uncertain glance.

"What's wrong?" asks George, noticing.

"How the heck do we use these things?" asks Atticus pointing to the obsidian in his crown.

"Yeah, I've only ever used the stones by accident," I admit.

The ancestors smile. "How could we forget to tell you?" says Flori. "You use your memories."

"Memories?" we all repeat.

"Yes," says Eve. "Maggie, what happened the first time you used my lapis lazuli?"

I think back to that first time it happened in the dormitory in the middle of the night. "Thorn had insulted my dad, then suddenly light burst out of the crown and knocked her down."

"See," says Sara Lisa. "She struck a memory that stirred in you a great deal of emotion, and your need to protect the memory of your father resulted in the blast. Wait, Wes!"

Wes's eyes are scrunched closed, and the stone is illuminated in his crown. Red light blasts at the plate of rolls, breaking the plate into a million pieces and sending rolls flying everywhere. Cornelius catches one in his crown, then impressively pops it in the air and takes a bite. "Scrumptious," he says.

"You have to be careful and try your best to control the stream by knowing the emotions around the memories you choose to you conjure. The blast comes when you remember something that brings you a lot of pain or anxiety. But watch." Sara Lisa gets a candle from the nightstand and sets it in the middle of the table. "Watch what happens when I remember the first time I saw my son Elliot's face." She touches her coronet with her fingers, and red light streams gently from her ruby to the candlewick. A flame erupts just as if it were lit with a match." Sara Lisa smiles at her work.

"Cool!" exclaims Atticus.

"So, since you are all new to using the stones, only use them when there is no other choice," says Justice.

All the kids agree to this even though we are all touching our crowns with newfound respect.

"But when trouble does come, don't be afraid to blast em' into next week." Gus winks.

Martha brings some blankets and makes beds for everyone on the floor. "We need more beds in here now that the Company is all together and we are staying here for longer stretches," she says.

Justice puts a hand on Martha's shoulder. "If all goes well, we'll be sleeping in the castle before long. And with no harm to befall us."

Martha smiles, but I can tell she doesn't know why Justice said this. I don't know either, but I'm too tired to find out.

Gus and Martha sleep in the bed since they are the oldest, and the rest of us sleep on the floor in blankets cuddled up with the warmouths and Horsemen. However, the Horsemen do not sleep but stay awake to keep watch.

I nestle between Calysta and Eve. Magnus rests on my chest, and Felixus hoots softly from a rafter. The sound of breath becomes heavy as everyone drifts off to sleep. Even amidst the most dangerous time I've ever lived in, my heart is about to burst.

This is family.

Chapter 33:
The Secret Hideaway

We head out at nightfall. Calysta is on the back of Cornelius, Atticus is on the back of Henry. We all agreed it would be best for them to ride since they are just getting well. I walk happily between Sara Lisa and Eve, the Horsemen's tails swinging before us. Wes and Jack follow.

I have no idea how even to begin looking for McShanihan but any chance to walk with this crew is a blessing in my book.

"Is there *anything* we should be watching for?" asks Atticus.

"Everything," says Eve.

"Yes, Brumbletide will use any means to get our attention and lead us to the right path."

This response didn't help at all. How are we supposed to examine *everything*?

"Do we at least know what we are walking toward?" asks Jack.

"No," replies Eve.

"You'll know it when you see it, children," says Sara Lisa.

The lampposts of Downtown Ipswich give it the same romantic glow that it had the night I ran away from home. It really is such a lovely town. If only there weren't a wicked monstrosity after it. I wonder how many people in Little Ipswich have made some sort of deal with Emily. I know it has to be a ton. It may not be only royals we are dealing with but *all* of Little Ipswich. After all, the castle has strong ties to the town. St. Michelle's hospital alone is steeped in Emily, and even the street I grew up on, Everly Drive, was named after Michelle Everly—it's everywhere!

We approach the bridge, where twice now I have had Brumbletide experiences. Once on top of the bridge, when words from Pippin's Puzzle started coming out of the sea, and another underneath the bridge, when Pippin himself came face to face with me and told me to get a move on it. The Horsemen trot over the bridge, and we follow. Unable to help myself, I stop and lean over the rail, listening and watching.

"Maggie?" says Eve, stopping to see what I'm doing.

"It was here where I heard the words form Pippin's Puzzle the night I ran away to find Dad. And then Pippin visited me underneath it when everyone had been kidnapped. There must be something about this spot."

Eve comes up beside me, crossing her arms on the railing. "Ah, the Lux Sea. A vast mystery connecting realms in a way that only it knows. You know, we could hear this world now and then from it in Brumbletide. Even people we didn't know who they were. We'd be sailing or in The Resplendent, and suddenly, voices would whisper—almost ring—from the sea. We can take a look. Everyone!"

The Horsemen and Sara Lisa bring the other kids over. Eve tells them to check below and around the bridge for anything unusual. Everyone searches thoroughly, and the Horsemen even go into the water to look.

"Nothing that we can see," says Cornelius. "We should probably keep going."

I'm a little embarrassed but agree with everyone that we should continue down the path to Little Ipswich the town. We will be coming up on my neighborhood soon, and I hope no one wants to stop to look there. Thankfully, we pass by, and no one says anything, but I have a haunting feeling that we may miss something by not looking on Everly Drive. We walk along the Ipswich wall to the edge of town where there is a dense forest. Wes starts to skip when it comes into view. He and I would always play in this forest when we were little.

"I miss this place, Maggie," Wes says. "Remember how much we played here? Remember the forts we built? Remember the tree house?"

"The In Between," says Sara Lisa.

All of us kids look sideways at the wood. *Is this* the infamous In Between where Sheba and the Whispers supposedly lived? It's a regular forest, and it's almost in my backyard.

"Oh, it's different than I imagined," says Calysta.

"Very *ordinary*," I add.

"Of course," says Sara Lisa. "Where else do you think extraordinary things are found?"

None of us says anything. If the others are thinking what I'm thinking, it's that Emily and Brumbletide are far from ordinary and if someone is looking for something extraordinary, those would be good places to look.

Eve watches us, amused. "Come on, let's go see what we can find."

In the forest, absolutely nothing is out of the ordinary with lots of trees, a path that can't decide if it will let people take it or not, blocking itself here and there with logs and thick brush. Birds chirp, flying from tree to tree. It may be ordinary, but I loved it when Wes and I would come play in the wood. Even on the hottest summer days, the leaves of the trees domed us in keeping us cool. It felt like we were visiting nature's palace and she was kindly allowing us to rest in her for a while. I remember building a treehouse with Wes a few summers ago. Every day, Wes would look up "how to build a safe treehouse" on the internet, and each morning, for weeks, we would search for supplies, stealing them from Dad when we couldn't find what we needed in the woods.

"We'll be coming up on the treehouse Wes and I built one summer. It was such a project—I can't believe we pulled it off."

"You should've had me help," says Atticus.

"You were never home. Always at Emily."

"Oh, yeah."

"Yeah, as fabulous as Emily is, you can't beat things like building a treehouse in the woods with your little brother. I actually miss seeing all of mine. I didn't think I would," says Calysta sounding melancholy. She has many siblings.

I put my arm around Wes's shoulders as we walk, relieved he is with us. Because of my shenanigans, he ended up alone with our mother for a while and then stuck in the dungeon with nothing to eat or drink for days on end. I hate that everyone was locked up, but I am thankful Wes wasn't alone down there. The memories seem to bring with them anxious feelings, and I let go of Wes's shoulders and cross my arms tightly in front of me.

"Is it me, or is this place starting to give you guys the creeps?" asks Calysta nervously.

"There is something about it," says Jack wearily.

Soon, the hodge-podge treehouse made of boards and branches of various sizes and types is just ahead in a dense patch of firs. Wes and I built it there precisely because the "hedge" of firs would hide our treehouse from the world. Our secret hideaway.

"Blimey, my skin is crawling," says Wes.

"Mine too, mate," says Jack. "Let's approach the treehouse cautiously."

"I don't know why, but I want to run around the wood! As fast as I can," says Atticus bouncing as he walks. "Like I've had twenty Fizzy Pops."

We have reached the bunch of firs, and Wes and I pull back some brush to show everyone our "fine" craftsmanship. The treehouse is still there, exactly as we left it. Dad's metal ladder still leans against the entryway. But something is vastly different from before.

"Great Scott! Do you see that?" breathes Jack.

"Incredible!" exclaims Calysta.

"Why haven't I seen it here before?" I ask, bewildered.

The treehouse Wes and I built a few summers back was in an ordinary beech—nothing magical or miraculous about it. But now, our shabby treehouse is stuck inside none other than the Silver Birch, the enchanted Silver Birch of the Forest Between the Worlds.

"It was here all along, friends," says Cornelius. "Magic is often right under our nose, but we refuse to see it."

I scrunch my nose, still grinding my teeth—is the tree doing this to me? Cornelius's statement is rather harsh. I think I would have wanted to see it back then, but I didn't even know to look!

Calysta screams, Wes and Jack yell and duck, and Atticus darts out of the firs in the other direction. Even the Horsemen rear up a little when a thunderous roar blows out of the treehouse.

"What the bloody hell was that?" yells Atticus, poking his head through the wall of firs.

The treehouse window displays a spectacular blue coronet as King Mortimer McShanihan pokes his head out. His long grey beard drops down like Rapunzel's hair. "Hello, friends!" he beams as if nothing at all extraordinary was happening in the world.

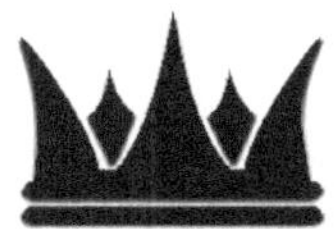

Chapter 34:
Ominous

"King McShanihan! What are you doing in our treehouse?" Wes exclaims.

"It's a remarkable treehouse," he replies from the window.

"Thank you," Wes replies proudly.

"What are you doing in it? We've needed you!" I yell.

"Have you needed me? Or did you need this?" He throws the Scepter of the Seven to Henry, who catches it, looking delighted. Always a strange look for Henry.

"Wonderful! It will be nice to sleep in a proper bed again," says Anastasia.

"I see you have some long-lost friends with you." Mcshanihan's eyes twinkle at Eve and Sara Lisa.

"Mortimer," Eve says kindly, and she and Sara Lisa curtsy.

"So good to have you in our realm, your majesties, perilous though it may be."

"Happy to be here," Sara Lisa says charmingly.

Welling with rage, I find it incredibly difficult to control my words. "You up and left us when we needed your help most! And you've just been up here in our treehouse the whole time? Hiding! What's wrong with you?!"

"Maggie!" scolds Eve.

"It's the Scepter," says Henry calmly. "We need to put it away so she can calm down."

"Do no such thing," says Sara Lisa. "You won't be able to change back without it, and Maggie and the children must learn to control the Scepter and not let it control them."

"I'm fine!" I yell.

"Yes, a real peach," replies Sara Lisa flatly.

"Sounds like you have some others in there with you," Eve calls up to McShanihan.

"Indeed," says a woman's lofty voice, and Sheba starts down the ladder in human form. Her friends, men who can transform into a wolf and a bear, follow her down the ladder. The Whispers.

"What are they doing here?" asks Atticus sharply. The Scepter is getting to all of us. Wes is centered in front of the Horsemen, asking to touch it.

"Come up, everyone. The Birch has calming properties. We will work with the Scepter in a while. Come up, come up!" McShanihan waves jovially.

Sheba takes Eve's hands and touches her forehead to hers affectionately. They have a special bond between them ever since

Sheba rescued Eve from having a hole drilled into her head when she used to be insane. "You look well," Sheba says to Eve just before she and the other Whispers melt into animal form. The ferocious tiger, stoic wolf, and massive bear disappear into the woods.

"Wow, I've never seen it happen so close up!" Calysta breathes.

We all climb the ladder to the treehouse. It screeches and creeks under our feet, making the skin of all those affected by the Scepter crawl. We groan. But the minute we step into the treehouse, there is a great deal of relief just as McShanihan said.

The treehouse is exactly as Wes and I left it—empty except for two lawn chairs we found in a neighbor's trash, some binoculars of Dad's that he never knew were borrowed, and a stack of Wes's comics and my Charlotte St. Pierre novels. Sara Lisa sits in my lawn chair and thumbs through one. "You fancy these, Maggie? I'm always looking for a good read. Magic ones!"

"Even with all the magic going on around you?" asks Jack.

"Oh, yes. After all, if one follows the magic in books long enough, it always leads to The Magic. Though only few will find it."

A flash of guilt washes over me. I love to read. Have I never found it? "Yes, Sara Lisa. They are about a poor girl who discovers new worlds through her bookshelf. Come to find out, all those lead to one big world."

"Ha! See!" Sara Lisa tells Jack who smiles.

We are all stuffed into the small treehouse. Sara Lisa and Eve are in the lawn chairs, McShanihan and all the kids are cross-legged on the plank floor. The Horsemen wait down on the ground letting the Scepter change them back into human form.

McShanihan addresses us all. "Now, we have five children, a bartender, a baker, a Queen, a Snickerling, a few warmouths, Six of Pippin's Chosen Seven, and three Horsemen going up against Tritch Anguis and the Einsreich."

"Right," us kids reply sadly.

"Wrong!" exclaims McShanihan. We all jolt.

"We have five children, a bartender, a baker, a Queen, a Snickerling, a few warmouths, Six of Pippin's Chosen Seven, and three Horsemen going up against Tritch Anguis, the Einsreich, and anyone in Little Ipswich who has the wicked spirit of Michelle fighting to stay alive through their hearts."

We all cringe at the news that's gone from bad to incredibly worse.

"Michelle's spirit in the hearts? What do you mean?" asks Calysta.

Eve speaks. "Any heart that isn't for Pippin and Brumbletide, Michelle can dwell in and make them part of his army. Hence, he has done everything in his power to hide Pippin and the true Brumbletide from Little Ipswich all these years."

"How absolutely tragic!" moans Calysta.

"It's impossible then!" I exclaim, defeated. "That's not only the royals of Emily—but *everyone* in Little Ipswich."

"We're outnumbered by tens of thousands," mutters Jack.

"Oh, buck up, children," says Sara Lisa. "You're bringing us all down even amid the Silver Birch," she waves her hands to the windows full of gleaming, leafy magical branches.

"Is there any chance at all that we can win, Your Majesty?" asks Calysta.

"Well that depends on how much faith you have in impossible things," says Eve, eyes twinkling.

"That's right," adds Sara Lisa. "And how well you can see things that aren't there."

My friends do not seem to find their words as frustrating as I do. I slump in my seat.

"Where do we start, King McShanihan?" asks Jack heavily.

"We will begin from the outside and work our way in."

"Outside the castle? We're outside it already, so that's good," I say.

"Precisely," says McShanihan. "Two by two, we will sort the marks."

"Sort the marks? What kind of marks?" asks Calysta.

"We have to sort those marked with Pippin's crest and those marked with Michelle's," Eve explains.

"What do they look like?" Calysta asks with wide eyes.

"Oh, you'll know them when you see them," says Sara Lisa.

"Where is it? I've been in Emily for years now and can't recall any mark on anyone," says Atticus.

"They, as well as you all here, have always borne one mark or the other, but the only way to see them is to use the stones," says Sara Lisa, pointing to the ruby in her coronet.

Calysta and Wes both touch their crowns with wonder.

"And not only can you not see the mark without the stones," says McShanihan, "but you must be able to control their power without blasting the mark bearer into oblivion."

My forehead creases. I will never be able to see a mark.

"You will all be trained in using your stones and controlling yourselves around the Scepter of the Seven before you go looking for a single mark," McShanihan consoles.

"Whew, that's a relief," breathes Calysta.

But I am still incredibly uneasy. I've already killed two people with the Scepter and blasted Thorn to the ground with Eve's stone—which I don't feel so bad about now.

Eve puts a hand on my back. "Everything in its time, Maggie."

"Quite right. And now it's time to learn." McShanihan says this in a non-ominous way, but I have an ominous feeling, nonetheless.

The grey-bearded king's expression hardens. "But I warn you never, under any circumstances, reveal your own marks to yourselves or each other. Never ever."

Ominous.

Chapter 35:
Remember

One by one, we descend the ladder down to the Horsemen who now have only two horse hind legs and long sweeping tails. I grind my teeth. My muscles become rigid.

"Friends, unfortunately, we must put the Scepter away for now so that the children can train to use their stones and not completely lose their minds due to the Scepter's pull." McShanihan tells the Horsemen.

"Understood, Your Majesty," says Cornelius placing the Scepter into the leather sack that McShanihan holds open. Calysta, Wes, Atticus, Jack, and I relax immediately.

Something strikes me. "I have a question. Why could I never see the mark on anyone when I had Eve's stone in my crown? I accidentally used its power a few times."

"We cannot see through other's stones, only our own, Maggie," Eve explains. "There are many tools that can be used and borrowed, good and evil, but there are some things that can only be used by their owner—the one destined to use it at the appointed time it is to be used."

I raise a brow. Sometimes, many times, none of this makes any logical sense.

"Everyone, line up," McShanihan commands.

Jack, Wes, Calysta, Atticus, and I form a line side by side. McShanihan plucks some pinecones from the fir trees and ground and sets one in front of each of us. "Mind, heart, and touch. Remember those."

"Mind, heart, and touch," I hear Wes say under his breath.

"Remember. Remember your heart for the memory. Add physical touch," McShanihan instructs, touching his great blue coronet with two fingers. "Now, everyone, think of your worst day. A day that made you very angry or sad."

At once, blasts of vivid red light the color of a cardinal explode all over the place. Terrified at their power, we all dive for the ground even as light escapes our crowns. Eve and Sara Lisa separate to dodge a beam shot from Jack's crown. McShanihan yelps as a bolt hits his foot. He beams and laughs with a little skip. "Whew! See how powerful memories can be? And left to their own, they get out of hand and do much harm. Let's rein them in, shall we?" He doesn't have to find anymore pinecones. All five of the ones he set down are right where he left them. Our beams of light didn't bother them in the least, though they bothered just about everything else.

McShanihan places two fingers on his crown. "This time touch your crown. This will hold the power inside when you think of the terrible memory."

We all put two fingers on our crowns. Dad's pale-white face comes into view again, his eyes wide and bloodshot seconds before his death. I feel the magic well up in the crown. There is pressure behind my fingers and on my head. I'm not sure how long the crown will hold without exploding.

"Now, think of one good thing that came from that terrible thing. There's always one," McShanihan instructs.

I try hard to get past Dad's white face and bloodshot eyes but all that comes to mind is his coffin going into the ground and Wes crying across the graveyard. More pressure builds in my crown. Beside me, a beam of light shines at the ground.

"Very good, Princess Calysta. Now, move the beam over to the pinecone."

Calysta directs the light to the pinecone and, after a few attempts, pushes it about a foot forward. More beams join hers, and in a moment, other pinecones have moved too.

Now added to the pressure of the memory is the pressure to perform. The blast is going to kill everyone.

"I've done it!" cries Wes. "Wow! Just like Depths of the Dimensions!"

Wes. He's done it! And he wouldn't be here learning how to use a magical crown if Dad wouldn't have died.

Red light blasts a bit more orderly this time out of the crown, and I move my head toward the pinecone. The light hits the pinecone, sending it rolling into the wood.

"Ah, a good start, Princess Maggie!" pipes McShanihan happily. "Practice makes perfect."

I scowl.

"This exercise will be more fun, but you must still use restraint. Remember to touch." McShanihan demonstrates with two fingers on his crown again. "Think of the best thing that has ever happened to you."

Beams of light shoot all over the place again sending the two-legged Horsemen off in different directions.

"I didn't say 'Simon says!'" McShanihan grins.

Like a line of soldiers, all place two fingers on our crowns.

"Your best memory," says McShanihan.

I remember Eve's first embrace. My crown wells with magic, warm and cheerful this time.

"Now, *feel* the memory. Indulge in its glory," McShanihan instructs.

Light gracefully shines in beams on the ground from all of our crowns.

"The pinecones," McShanihan says softly.

When we direct the light to the pinecones, they lift off the ground and into the air. I smile, happy that this time was much easier.

"Well done! Well done!" exclaims McShanihan. Eve, Sara Lisa, and the Horsemen applaud heartily.

We run through the exercises several more times, setting things in the trees and bringing them down again. Atticus, Wes, and Jack all blunder here and there, blowing up pinecones completely or blasting branches from trees. I hate to say I'm glad since my bad memories still seem to bring with them more power than necessary.

When McShanihan brought out the brown leather sack that we all knew held the Scepter, a groan growls from the kids.

"Oh, come on, young ones, it's not that bad," says Sara Lisa.

"And you'll be so relieved when you see how easy it is to control," adds Eve.

Holding the sack in his hands, McShanihan, paces slowly in front of us. "With great power, comes great pride. That is what is taking all of you over."

But that doesn't seem so bad. It's good to take pride in things.

"And with great pride," add McShanihan solemnly, "comes great destruction."

That escalated quickly. Really?

"Since the Scepter is one of the most powerful weapons ever created, naturally, great temptation will come with it. Can anyone guess how to solve this dilemma?"

No one raises their hand or says anything. But suddenly, Wes lets loose the longest and loudest fart I've ever heard and immediately starts laughing uncontrollably, his cheeks burning red. Atticus and Jack are dying with laughter too. Calysta grins at me in surprise.

McShanihan, too, is doubled over laughing. "Young Prince Wesley, you're brilliant! You got it—humiliation. Humiliation is the antidote."

When the laughter has calmed down, McShanihan tells us to think of our most humiliating moment when he takes the Scepter out of its sack.

"Whenever you feel the Scepter getting to you, place yourself in your moment of humblement. You'll find you will have to try less and less the more you get used to the exercise. Everyone ready?"

"Ready," we reply.

McShanihan removes the Scepter from the bag, and I immediately wince with nervous tension and the urge to grab the Scepter out of his hands.

"Remember your humiliation!" shouts McShanihan.

I press my eyes closed and think. My first time to Emily pops into mind when Mum, Wes, and I were the only ones not dressed in royal garments. I think of all the stupid and terrible things I did with the Scepter before. I squeeze my eyes tighter, remembering everyone climbing all the way to the flag of George Tower except for me—I couldn't even get going. I think of everyone's horrified faces when I beat Monica Spivey senseless in Gottfrig's Grab. And just as McShanihan said, the anxiety fades immensely. The rest of the anxiousness and pulling disappears completely. I open my eyes to Eve smiling. She winks. "You've got it, my love."

"Well done," says King McShanihan.

Chapter 36:
The Mark

To my disdain, McShanihan did not come with us back to the Boggletrice Company. He stayed in the treehouse! But he did send us back with the Scepter, and neither the ancestors nor the Horsemen seemed upset that he stayed behind.

It has been a whole day since our training with McShanihan. Jericho and Martha have made yet another wonderful feast, which we are indulging in at the moment. The Scepter is in its leather sack and back in the mouth of the ugly, non-human, non-animal head on the wall above the fireplace. Magnus is asleep on its nose, enjoying the warmth of the fire below, which Fergus is curled up in front of.

George, Flori, Soleil, and Justice returned with a horrible report from Emily. It is a one-to-one ratio of royal to Einsreich in the castle, and Tritch Anguis is feeding Thorn every word to get the public on their side. They say that the Einsreich is the future of Little Ipswich's greatness and something to embrace as equal to a regular Emily royal. They even say that Pippin will be displeased with them if they do not accept the Einsreich as equal to themselves. The whole thing makes me want to puke.

Felixus settles on Justice's head as he pours us all some Bubblegin. "As Mortimer said, we will pair up two by two to sort the marks."

"Which we still don't know how to do," I interrupt.

"Yes, you do, Princess," Justice replies, sounding annoyed. My cheeks burn.

"We will go through the town. Anyone with Michelle's mark, leave them be. Anyone with Pippin's, do whatever you must to get them to come back here with you."

"Here? How in the world will everyone fit in this small cottage?" asks Calysta.

"Easily," says George bluntly.

"We will get started first thing in the morning. Who will go with whom?" Justice asks the table.

Hooooo! Felixus adds his two cents.

I look at Eve hoping she will be my partner. She smiles but shakes her head. "I'm afraid it's best for us to go with someone close to our own ages."

"Eve's right," says Flori. "Less suspicious."

"Want to go with me, Maggie?" asks Calysta.

"Sure."

Wes pairs with Atticus, Jack with Soleil (noticed by me that they are *not* close to the same age), Gus with Martha, Lenore with Eve, Sara Lisa with Justice, George with Henry, Anastasia with

Cornelius, and Flori with the warmouths—yes, the warmouths. Nothing says inconspicuous more than a little queen wearing a coat with many pockets and flocked by a bunch of winged animals.

With our partners chosen and our bellies full, we nestle into the blankets and cuddle up to the warmouths for a good night's sleep. Magnus has moved his spot to my leg and is already snoring heavily.

I am awakened by Fergus's heavy panting and wet licks. The smell of bacon, cinnamon rolls, and coffee fills the cottage. Calysta and Jack are already at the table eating breakfast. I feel a twinge of jealousy when Jack nudges Calysta, grinning because of some joke he's told, and she laughs in response. *Stop it, Maggie.*

"Morning, Maggie," says Calysta brightly.

"Morning," I reply, pouring some coffee.

Eve pushes a plate of bacon toward me. "Eat, Maggie. Today is a big day."

"Where do we start?" I ask anyone.

Soleil swallows a pinch of cinnamon roll. "We were talking about it and have come up with designated areas for everyone. We were thinking you and Calysta could take Dragon Street."

Eve leans in. "That's where I lived."

I shrug. "Fine with me, I guess."

After breakfast, we all get ready to go. Atticus and Wes will go to our old neighborhood, Ipswich Hills. "Avoid your house at all costs," Eve warns Wes. "Your mother is in a bad way."

Soleil and Jack are going to the In Between. Eve and Lenore are going to Victor's Spoil, the rich part of town. Gus and Martha are taking Downtown Ipswich. Justice and Sara Lisa are going to the hospital. Cornelius and Anastasia will take the businesses on the outskirts, George and Henry the police and fire station. Flori is taking the warmouths to the schools.

"Two will go out and then the next two will go about five minutes after them so we aren't all leaving at once," says Justice.

Hoo hoooo

"Flori, you all will go last since you will draw the most attention," George says to Flori, Magnus, Fergus, Teddy, and Theary.

"Won't it be strange, you walking into the school with all of them?" asks Calysta.

"Yes, Princess, it's what I'm countin' on, matter a fact. The children will go wild over these fellows, and the teachers should be more than happy to take a break for the day while I give the kids a show." She winks. Felixus is perched on her should, her beaver, Teddy, is bundled under her arm. Theary is in the palm of her three-fingered hand, and Fergus pants happily by her side. Zelda the white dragon pouts on the rug. She was told she couldn't go because a dragon is just too much for the townspeople to take.

"Alright, Maggie and Calysta, come along. You two are first," Justice waves us to the front of the line.

Eve kisses my forehead. "Be safe. Keep keen watch around you at all times."

"Yes, ma'am."

"Don't forget your stones," she nods to our crowns. "The happy memory will show the sign."

"We won't forget," says Calysta.

With that, Calysta and I step through the fireplace into the pub. Gus is waiting on the other side. "Take the back door, Queenie. Dragon Street is straight across the field. You can see some of the chimneys from here."

"Okay, thanks, Gus."

"Be careful, you two," Gus pleads.

"We will," says Calysta.

Gus lets us out the back door, and Calysta and I cut through the grass to Dragon Street, about a football field away.

"I'm so glad we changed into jeans. I hate when weeds tickle my feet," says Calysta.

I laugh but understand.

The houses on Dragon Street are the poorest in town. I've always known about the area but have never been. The only people that go there are the people who live there. Calysta and I wade through the tall grass and weeds all the way to someone's back garden. Trudging through, we both keep our eyes down looking for snakes, so we jump when a rattly voice calls to us from the house's back porch.

"Toppa the mornin' to ya."

"Blimey! I thought it was a snake!" Calysta yelps, clutching her chest.

The voice belongs to an old woman in a rocking chair. "You two lost your way?" The woman is ancient but has a kind smile. She rocks in her chair bundled in many layers of clothing. Elderly people are always cold.

"I don't think so," I tell the woman. "We just wanted to meet the people on this street. We never come out this way."

"What are those for?" she asks, nodding to our crowns.

"We're academy students," Calysta tells her. "Is this your house?"

"Oh, yeah. Lived here fifty years, I have."

"You check for a sign. I'll keep talking," Calysta whispers.

"The academy, eh? Emily Castle," the woman croaks. The rocking chair's creaking sounds much like her voice.

I touch my crown and remember when Calysta and I first met in The Resplendent. Warm red light shines on the woman but she doesn't flinch—doesn't seem to notice in the least.

"Yes, we enjoy going to school there. We're out on a project for Hospitality."

"How nice. Yes, Emily is the jewel of Ipswich, it is. It'll save us all one day."

It takes all I have not to scream.

"Yes, yes, Emily is our savior. I believe it! When the time is right, King Michelle and Emily will save us all."

In the light of the stone, the woman's old, wrinkled, yet kind face has been completely taken over by a serpent's head. When she speaks, a forked tongue flicks between words.

"Maybe so," says Calysta, looking at me. I shake my head.

"They will, I believe it! They'll save us all," she slithers.

"Well, nice to meet you, ma'am. We'll see you around."

"Alright, dears. Stay in school. You won't do better than Emily."

Calysta gives a little laugh. "Alright, see you."

We step through her garden to the street.

"What did you see?" Calysta asks.

"Her head became a snake's head!"

"Creepy!" Calysta's face scrunches in horror.

"You do the next one so you can see."

We cross the street. No one is outside, so we knock on the door. A tall man with a white undershirt answers. "Selling something? I don't want any. He goes to close the door."

"No sir!" I say quickly. "We aren't selling anything. Have you seen our dog? We've lost him. A little white, puffy thing."

"No," the man scowls. "Haven't seen any dogs. What are those about?" He points a long, skinny finger at our crowns.

"We're academy students," I say.

His scowl deepens. "Bah, all a bunch of rubbish. All of it. Get out while you're young. Better to go with no education at all than to get it from that place."

I look to Calysta who shakes her head, eyes huge.

"Noted, sir. Thank you. We'll be on our way."

The man closes the door, and Calysta and I hurry off into the street.

"The snake's head?" I ask.

"No! His skin was ripped off, and blood was everywhere!"

"Blimey!"

"I don't want to talk to anyone else if that's what we're going to see," Calysta pants as we continue down Dragon Street.

"Me either, but there must be people with Pippin's mark here too. I'll be ready with the stone this time when they open the door, so we aren't there any more than necessary."

"Good idea," Calysta says with a shiver.

We wearily step up the walkway of the house next door to the bloody-faced man. My fingers are on my crown, and my mind is on Eve saying, "I hear you are a daughter of mine."

Calysta knocks. After several seconds, a mother of many children comes to the door with a baby on her hip and several kids crowded around her legs.

I yelp.

All of them, the mother, the baby, and each of the children, have only gaping black holes for eyes.

"I-I'm sorry, ma'am," I manage.

"Spoiled Emily brats!" she scowls before slamming the door in our face.

"Wasn't pretty, I take it?" Calysta mutters.

"Wasn't pretty," I say, clutching my chest.

House by house, we look for anyone who has Pippin's crest, but we find only Michelle's hideous sign on everyone. The town is much worse off than I ever would have thought. Is there anyone who will fight with us?

There aren't many houses left now. Calysta and I are traumatized by all the sights of horror that are Michelle's crest. How much more can we possibly take? At least none of us has to sleep alone tonight in the cottage. There are sure to be nightmares.

Taking several deep breaths, we hesitate before knocking on the next door, but the door opens startling us yet again. We both gasp and jolt. Another old woman, crotchety and wrinkled, glares at us with beady eyes. "I've been watchin' you two goin' door to door. You go home now! Dragon Street's no place for children to be wanderin' alone, and the house next door is the deadliest door you'll knock on. Whatever you do, do not go there!" She shouts the last line with squinted eyes.

I look at Calysta whose fingers are still on her crown. She shakes her head. The woman bears Michelle's crest.

"Killed children—many children! Children just like you two. Stole a bunch of money from their home and went to get away with it. Police caught him in the forest. Made some sorta deal with the devil—only reason he's out here on our street, and I have the misfortune of having to live inside with my doors and windows shut and bolted."

"Alright, ma'am. Sorry to bother you," says Calysta. "We'll be on our way."

"Go home now! Run along back to where you came from. Heed my words!" The door shuts with a thud.

"She sure talks a lot about watching out for danger for someone with a massive axe in her neck!" Calysta says, and we both laugh an awkward laugh.

When we are in the street again, we both stare at the house next door—the house of the child murderer. An eerie silence falls over us. Should we really not go? We are supposed to sort everyone. No one said anything about if people were known to be dangerous or not.

The curtains in the window in the murderer's house move a little and a young boy appears. He sees us and then is gone.

Calysta gasps. "Did you see that?"

"What in the world is he doing in there? Did the murderer catch him?" I say worriedly.

"I don't know of any other explanation. We've got to save him, Maggie!"

Here we go again. Why do I always seem to end up in situations that put an end to the plan even before it begins?

"Alright. How? The murderer is probably inside with him."

We decide to venture down the street a little ways in case the nosy neighbor lady is watching us and then turn around and make our way back to the window of the murderer's house, crouching low in the few back gardens we have to pass en route. After a few minutes of anxious creeping, we are huddled beneath the murderer's window, waiting. If he appears again, we can somehow let him know that we are here. If the murderer comes, we can run and think of something else. No wait, the stones! We can blast him with the stones!

But no boy.

Calysta rustles the bush we are hiding under. No boy.

"We've got to get his attention somehow," I whisper.

Calysta throws a pebble at the window. We both watch, still as stone and silent.

It isn't long after this that the face of the boy appears in the window. He is small with crooked glasses and disheveled hair. The murderer has obviously not been feeding him; he is skinny and there are dark circles under his eyes.

Calysta throws another pebble and the boy's large, sunken-in green eyes shift to us. We freeze.

The boy looks out into the neighborhood to see if anyone is watching before pointing to the door. Calysta and I get up and meet him at his entryway. His little weary head pokes out the cracked door, looking at us like we are aliens, and he doesn't know if we will do him harm or good.

"Hello," I say quietly. "We've come to see if you are alright."

His lips part. He looks relieved—almost hopeful. "Do you want to come inside?"

"Is anyone home with you?" Calysta asks.

"Only me."

Calysta and I exchange an apprehensive glance. The murderer may be gone but he will return at some point and we have to be gone when he does.

"Alright, only for a minute," I say. Calysta shoves me. I shrug in reply.

"What she means to say is we are here to rescue you," Calysta tells him pressingly.

"Oh, thank you very much," the boy replies calmly. "Come in."

He opens the door, and Calysta and I enter the dark, empty house. It is clean but only because it is almost entirely empty. There is no furniture, no sign of any reading or hobby, nothing except the things that come with a house when it's built, a pillow and blanket on the floor, and a pitcher of water and loaf of white bread on the counter.

"How long have you been here?" Calysta asks in surprise at the house.

The boy looks up, trying to recall. "Years now. I'm not sure how many."

"Years!" Calysta exclaims. "Where is the murderer? Is he coming back?"

The boy's shoulders slump as if with sudden disappointment he thought might not come. "Who told you?"

"The woman next door. She warned us not to come here because a murderer lives here. We weren't going to, but then we saw you in the window."

The boy is gloomy as if he has been sad for so long he has forgotten how to be happy. "I am the murderer."

Calysta and I both gawk at the boy, stunned.

"You?" I say.

"Maggie!" Calysta shouts, her fingers on her crown. "Look! Shine your light on him."

Like a knee-jerk reaction, my fingers dart to my crown, and I think of Eve. The boy watches us curiously now, but on his head, poking out of his disheveled hair, are a pair of two grand and gleaming white antlers.

Chapter 37:
The Murderer

"You're lying," I say. "The real murderer is making you say that."

The boy deflates, and his shoulders slump even more. Dragging his feet, he goes to the blanket on the floor and sits, drawing his legs into his arms.

"There is no *real murderer*. Besides me, that is. I am the only one who lives here, and I am a murderer. My whole family is gone because of me."

Calysta's solemn face softens, and she sits down on the blanket by the boy. "Why would you say such a thing? Is your family really gone?"

The boy nods, his eyes watering. "Yes, and it's all because of me. There was a terrible storm—I love terrible storms. I don't know why; I've always been fascinated by lightning and powerful wind. That storm that night was the best there'd ever been. Course, Mum and Dad thought it was the worst there'd ever been, and they ended up being right because of what happened. I wanted to go outside to watch it. She'd usually let me. But this time Mum said no, it was too dangerous. The power had already gone out in the house, and she lit candles in all the rooms. I never spoke back to Mum, so I didn't pitch a fit or anything. But I just had to go. I had to go out in the storm! I don't know why—I don't why I'm like this!" He claps his hands over his face and rocks back and forth on his bum.

Calysta puts a hand on his shoulder. "Come now, mate. We all do stuff like that now and then."

"But we don't kill our families over it," I remind her.

Sobs muffle out of his hands that are pressed hard into his face. "*But I killed them!* I couldn't control myself. I went to the loo, closed the door, and climbed out the window. I ran off into the wood to be in the storm. It was glorious." He bursts into more sobs.

Calysta and I don't say anything, but I know we are both braced for when the part about the murder comes.

The boy brings his hands away from his wet, puffy face. "What I didn't know, was that while I was having the time of my life, Mum had brought everyone—Dad and all six of my brothers and sisters—to the attic to watch the storm. She did it just for me. I know it, because she's taken me up there to watch when the storms were too bad to sit outside on the porch. But when I climbed out of the window, the curtain must have caught the flame of the candle Mum lit in the bathroom. The fire spread fast. My whole family was trapped in the attic because of the fire, and it was too high to jump." His voice cracks, and he presses his eyes closed as tightly as they will go, shaking his head like he is trying to shake the memory out.

At this, I drop to his side as well. "It's not your fault."

"Yes, it is! I murdered them!"

"No, you didn't! It was an accident. A tragic accident!" Calysta is crying now too. She comes from a large family herself.

"I went straight to the police and turned myself in. They put me in jail where I belong but then came the next day and told me I couldn't stay because they could tell it was an accident. But it was murder, I tell you. Only murder could feel like this inside! I belong in prison for the rest of my life. But the sheriff brought me here. He comes by to check on me and bring me food. Far more than I deserve."

Calysta and I are speechless. This poor boy who can't be more than Wes's age has been living in misery for who knows how long. Calysta wraps an arm around his shaking shoulders. "What's your name, mate?"

"Ernie."

"Ernie, what if you had a chance to do a lot of good for a lot of people?"

He looks at her curiously. "I-I'd do it. But no one can take the sight of me anymore, and I don't blame them."

"Well, your story has been embellished a bit outside these walls. Come with us! We work for Pippin and the Boggletrice

Company." Calysta holds her hand out to Ernie for him to shake, but all he can do is say, "Pippin? The Stag?"

"You know Pippin?" I ask.

"Oh, yes. Dad told us loads of stories about him. He'd tell 'em at bedtime or when he was driving us someplace. Fantastic creature. But he's not real, is he?"

Calysta and I beam at Ernie.

"As real as you are," I say.

He smiles curiously and finally shakes Calysta's hand.

"Come on," Calysta says, pulling Ernie up, and then the three of us are off, careful to leave the house inconspicuously so the nosy neighbor lady won't see us. There are two houses left on Dragon Street to sort. We take Ernie with us. No one expects that *he* is the "murderer" they've all been terrified of. He jumps when we are snapped at by a mean man with scorpions for hair and watches in wonder as we are startled yet again by what he sees as a humble professor, but Calysta and I see as a man with an exposed bleeding brain. The next house wasn't much better, a skeleton so dry that flakes of bone shook off the young woman like snow.

With all the houses checked, the three of us hightail it as fast as we can through the field to Lazy Jug.

Chapter 38:
The Pippin of the Stories

Ernie is speechless with bewilderment as he follows Calysta and me through the fire into the Boggletrice Company headquarters.

"Who do we have here?" says Ignatius as we pass through.

"His name is Ernie. He's got Pippin's mark!" says Calysta.

When we step out of the fire, everyone else is already back. Every head is turned to Ernie. Two fingers are on every crown.

Ernie yelps as he is sniffed from head to toe by Fergus and Zelda.

"They're strange but safe," I tell him.

Now, all faces beam at Ernie. He squirms with all the eyes on him.

"Look at those brilliant points," Flori says proudly. "Pippin's mark."

"Where are the others?" I ask. Ernie is the only one not part of the original group that left this morning.

"There were none!" exclaims George, throwing his arms, obviously still bothered by it.

"Not one!" pipes Flori. The warmouths, too, ruffle their feathers and fur, flustered. "Not one in that damned school. There musta been three hundred kids—not one!"

Justice comes and brings Ernie to a seat at the table. "Are you hungry, son?"

Ernie licks his lips and his eyes widen at the stacks of hot sandwiches before him. "Yes, sir."

"By all means, help yourself," Justice tells him, loading a plate with sandwiches and pouring him a glass of Bubblegin. "Eat! Eat up while you tell us about yourself." Justice is absolutely joyful.

But just as Ernie is about to take a huge bite of a melty ham and cheese, he stops and lowers the sandwich. His shoulders return to their usual slump.

Justice looks curiously at Calysta and me.

"I don't think he can bear to eat, King Justice," says Calysta.

"It's a terribly tragic story. Let us tell it, Ernie. Try to eat. It's alright, mate," I say.

Ernie nods, looking like someone has delivered him a birthday cake made of dung. He doesn't eat.

Calysta and I recount the horror as delicately as possible to the Boggletrice Company, who listen with gasps, clutched chests, gaping mouths, and oh-my-dear-boy!s.

By the end of the story, Ernie is in tears all over again, but this time surrounded by warm embraces, consoling hands, gentle words, and even licks from furry warmouths, which, against his will, brings a smile to his face.

"My dear boy, no one in the room is a stranger to regret," Eve tells him, wiping his tears. "And where there is regret, there is always tragedy. But, Prince Ernie," Ernie is caught off guard at Eve calling him prince, "Pippin knows your name. You bear his mark and have a lot of work to do."

"Important work, young man," adds Flori.

Soleil clears her throat grabbing our attention. "I would just like to quickly insert that when all is said and done, I'll show you how to *really* have fun with lightning. I know a fellow Whitescale when I see one." She winks. Ernie's cheeks go pink.

Zelda rushes up, flies over everyone's head, and plunks her little dragon bum in Ernie's lap, panting happily. This makes us all laugh, and the atmosphere in the cottage lightens dramatically.

"Now, we have quite a story for *you*," Justice tells Ernie. "But please eat, son. You're wasting away."

This time, Ernie takes a big, blissful bite and then begins listening intently to every word told to him about Emily, Michelle, Pippin, Brumbletide, the Anguises, the Einsreich, and all of it. By the end of the story, Ernie is full and hiccupping, but his already pale face has lost even more color. I think, of all of us, Ernie has received the news the best, and that is probably because there is just about nothing worse than losing your family in a fire you caused.

Everyone watches Ernie for some reaction. He hasn't said a word this whole time. Ernie, however, looks at none of us. He seems to be processing it all, leaning back in his chair with his belly out. Suddenly, he sits up straight. "Have any of you heard the stories about the White Stag?"

Everyone nods or answers with "yes."

"My ole dad told us stories of Pippin the White Stag King. He was always up to peculiar things. Doesn't it seem like *all this* is one of those peculiar things?"

I watch as the Six grin and agree with Ernie.

"If this Pippin you are telling me about is the same Pippin of the stories, it's all gonna be alright. He's got tricks up his sleeve."

"Yes, sir, that's the spirit!" says Justice, beaming.

"But you've still got to be brave," adds George soberly. "There is a genuine possibility that a lot of blood will pour before the war ends."

"Who am I to turn my eyes from it?" says Ernie solemnly.

"By golly, everyone, I think we may be in the midst of a true warrior," says George, slapping Ernie on the back, causing him to burp.

Ernie's cheeks glow on his pale face.

"This calls for a toast," says Justice, filling everyone's glass with Bubblegin. When everyone has a glass of bubbly, crimson drink, Justice raises his own. "Who will do the honors?"

"I will this time." It's Soleil. She raises her glass high, her face lit with cheer. Everyone follows suit. "To the lovers of good storm." Soleil smiles at Ernie. "To the warriors, to the good, and to the Pippin of the stories."

"Hear, hear!" we all reply before sipping.

The Bubblegin tickles my tongue and throat just like the nagging thoughts tickling my brain and boring a hole into it. Where is this Pippin of the stories? Why hasn't he shown up lately? Why is he having *us* do all his bidding? I put my glass down, keeping my eyes on it as not to look into any other eyes in the room.

Who really is Pippin, anyway? How do we know it is his side we should be fighting on? Why have we all just blindly followed him? What if he isn't the only other option? What if Pippin isn't even good like we thought?

THE END

Brynn Miller, age 11

Brynn Miller, age 11